The Long-Timer Chronicles

Crazy Like Foxes

G. M. Lupo

Lupo Digital Services, LLC
Atlanta, GA

Copyright © 2024 by G. M. Lupo

All rights reserved. No part of this book may be reproduced, stored in a retrieval system or transmitted in any form or by any means without the prior written permission of the publishers, except by a reviewer, who may quote brief passages in a review.

First edition (Pocket Paperback).

The material in this work was originally published in 2007 as *The Longtimers* (ISBN 1-4241-8826-1). It was subsequently republished as *The Long-Timer Chronicles: Crazy Like the Foxes*, in 2012 (ISBN 978-0-9848913-1-3).

The graphic of the foxes on the cover of this work was created using an AI generator in Adobe Express. All other content, written or otherwise, is the original work of the author.

ISNI: 0000 0005 0315 9196

ISBN: 978-0-9981595-9-1. Published by Lupo Digital Services, LLC, Atlanta, Georgia (www.lupo.com). Printed in the United States of America.

Introduction

The writing process which yielded my first published novel *The Longtimers* began in 2006 with my attempt to create a work using techniques I developed posting articles on the Internet. My process was to compose short, one-shot, humorous narratives that I edited quickly and posted immediately without overthinking them.

The first scene I committed to writing had been rolling around in my head for more than twenty years, since I first imagined it in college. A woman enters an art museum, and stops at a painting from hundreds of years before that resembles her. A man says, "Absolutely stunning." The woman thanks him, and when he turns to clarify he's talking about the painting, he realizes she looks like the woman in the painting. He excuses himself and the woman is joined by her husband who says, "Still turning heads, I see."

This couple became Charles and Renee Fox, and my plan was to center the story around them and their chief adversary, named Bergeron. Then, on the very first page, Bergeron murders a prostitute who shares the same attributes as him and the Foxes, and as I developed her story, she came to totally dominate the book. This volume represents my efforts to reclaim the Foxes narrative, giving them their own novel in which to shine.

Whereas *Tales of Two Sisters* was crafted almost entirely from *The Longtimers* by simply repackaging Victoria and Allison's stories, *Crazy Like Foxes* reimagines the story which appeared in the original novel, adding a new character, Eleanor Goolsby (who takes on the name Rigby within the story), and splitting the focus between Renee and Charles and their children, Isabella, Nathaniel, Roland, and Katherine. Isabella and Nathaniel are additions who did not appear in my first attempt to spin off the Foxes story, and Isabella's story includes her daughter, Rani.

It is my pleasure to reintroduce the Foxes to readers. Enjoy!

Other Work by the Author

G. M. Lupo is the author of these works:

- *Another Mother*, originally published as *Worthy*
- *The Long-Timer Chronicles: Tales of Two Sisters*
- *Atlanta Stories: Reconstruction*
- *Words Words Words: Essays, Poetry, Stories*
- *Rebecca Too*
- *Atlanta Stories: Fables of the New South*

For new stories in development or to be added to the mailing list for future releases, visit the author's blog Raised by Wolves at http://gmlupo.com.

When Charles Met Renee

In the stories of our people, that have been handed down for many generations, it is told that our ancestors once wandered in the land of ice where nothing would grow, and food was scarce. They had been there many years, their numbers had dwindled, and the will of the people was low. Their leader Kanute stood before the Great Spirit and cried out for a sign from which they could gain solace.

One day, Kanute was out hunting when he spotted a fox seated before him. The Great Spirit rained down its light, surrounding the fox and when Kanute drew near to investigate, the fox ran ahead of him. Kanute followed and when the fox was many lengths away, it stopped and sat again, until Kanute was nearby, then moved away and waited for Kanute to follow. Kanute summoned those who were hunting with him and sent them to gather the tribe and have them come to where he was. Soon, all the people were with Kanute, who bade them to follow as the fox guided him.

For forty days and nights Kanute and the people followed the fox, and, at the end, Kanute tracked the fox to the top of a hill and before him, Kanute beheld a wondrous sight. The ice gave way to lush green fields, trees bearing fruit as far as the eye could see, and animals of all sizes. Kanute called for the people to join him and when they witnessed the sight, they cried out in joy over their blessings.

At the base of the hill, Kanute found the spirit had left the fox which lay dead. He removed the pelt then wrapped the fox in burlap and lit a large fire. Kanute placed the fox's body on the fire as an offering to the Great Spirit. The pelt he strung up between several poles to be carried as a standard for the tribe.

To this day the fox remains the guiding spirit of our people.

Outside the Metropolitan Museum of Art, a banner announcing a showing from painters of the Dutch Golden Age flutters in the wind. A tall, refined woman, with dark hair and vibrant green eyes, who appears to be no older than her late thirties, enters and heads toward the exhibit room featuring the collection. She carries herself with confidence, a slight smile suggesting a sense of satisfaction with who she is and how she got to where she is in life. For the better part of that life, at least among her closest acquaintances, she has been known as Renee, though publicly she has used many names throughout the years.

She enters the exhibit hall, scans the room, locates the object of her search, and moves toward the large painting of a dark-haired woman with green eyes, dressed in seventeenth century garb, sitting on an elegant chair. In every detail, she has the exact same face and physique as the woman now heading toward her. The date of the painting is the mid-1600s and the artist is Rembrandt van Rijn. The painting is entitled, "Madame Renard, seated."

A man stands before it, staring intently at the likeness. Without removing his eyes from the canvas, he speaks to no one in particular: "Absolutely stunning."

Renee turns to the man. "Why, thank you."

The man chuckles, then looks toward Renee. "Oh, I'm sorry, I was talking about—"

He stops when he sees her face then looks at the painting and then Renee.

"Excuse me."

He quickly moves on to a different section of the museum.

Amused by the exchange, Renee turns her eyes back to the painting.

From behind her comes a man's voice.

"Still turning heads, I see."

"Charlie!"

She turns and throws her arms around the man standing there, her husband, Charles Fox. He is a bit taller than her and has brown hair that's not quite shoulder length.

Renee pulls away and gives him a slight push. "How long have you been in town?"

"I came in a few days ago, but I didn't stay in town. I took a train up to Highland Falls for some hiking and just got back this morning."

"Well, you should have called." She links her arm into his. "See? I told you they'd have it."

"So, you did. I somehow knew you'd be here staring wistfully at it."

"It's quite possibly the best painting that's ever been done of me. Plus, Rembrandt was an absolute sweetheart. He said I reminded him of his wife."

They stroll around the exhibit room, examining the other paintings.

"I must have just missed you at the loft. I dropped my bags there and grabbed some coffee."

"What did you think of the improvements?"

"I hardly recognized the place. Definitely more to our tastes. When did the tenants leave?"

"Months ago. It seemed like the perfect time to come back and spruce up the place. How was Highland Falls?"

"Beautiful — great views of the Hudson. Sometimes it's nice to just get away from it all and these days it's getting harder to get away."

"Agreed."

"Oh. I ran into Katie in England. She says she's cast in a play that goes into rehearsals later this month, so she'll probably be staying with us."

"Well, Isabella's still in Frankfort with Rani, who says she's enjoying her latest tenure in university. Have you heard anything from Nathaniel?"

"He's been growing coffee in Kenya when he's not exploring Egypt. And Roland?"

"Still driving a cab in Australia."

"He realizes his sentence was lifted over a hundred years ago, right."

"He knows. I think he just likes it there."

"He's always been the homebody."

Renee stops and jumps in front of him. "Hey, I hear they have a collection of clothing from the Renaissance upstairs. We could go up and make fun of how much they got wrong."

"Sounds like a plan. Have you seen anyone in town?"

"Our kind of anyone? Not here, but while I was in Paris I caught up with Maxine."

Charles laughs. "Maxine. I've never seen anyone take to a city like she did to Paris."

"She deserves it."

"Yes she does. Has she heard from—?"

"No. Maxine says she hasn't heard from her since they were in Paris in the teens."

"You don't suppose she's still here, do you?"

Renee shrugs. "Somewhere, certainly."

"She'll turn up. Victoria knows how to take care of herself. She survived Bergeron after all."

"That I will never understand. I can barely stand being in the same city with him let alone the same house."

"Well, you know my thoughts on the matter."

She runs her hand over his stomach. "I certainly do."

Arriving at the historical clothing section, they stroll along while Renee examines each one closely.

"Someone's been doing his homework. Not much to complain about."

Charles points to one. "What does that remind you of?"

Renee touches her finger to her chin then shakes her finger. "That party at the de Medici's. We met Leonardo there."

"Pity he was only there to sketch the partygoers and wasn't allowed to mingle. I always wish I had more of an opportunity to pick his brain."

Renee examines the dress more closely. "Of course, they have the accessories all wrong." She looks around and spots an attendant. "Excuse me, Miss?"

"Yes ma'am." The attendant approaches.

"The accessories on this dress are wrong."

"I'm sorry?"

"The accessories. They're from a different time period than the dress."

"Ma'am, our curator is an expert in Renaissance fashions."

"I'm not debating your curator's expertise. I'm just saying this setup is wrong."

"Excuse me a minute."

The attendant steps away from them and gets on her cell phone.

"You've done it now." Charles speaks in a taunting manner. "They're bringing out the big guns."

Renee covers her mouth and giggles.

A few minutes later, a bald man with a salt and pepper beard, arrives and speaks to the attendant. She points at Renee and the man steps over to her.

"I'm Stanley Maxwell. I designed this display, and I understand you have a complaint."

"Not so much a complaint as an observation." Renee steps toward the dress in question and points toward the top. "The stitching and frills on this dress put it clearly within the reign of Lorenzo de Medici. The first one, that is, the one they call the Magnificent, though, in my estimation, he wasn't at all. But that's a story for another day." She indicates the jewelry. "These accessories are from a much later period, the period of Duke Lorenzo two generations later." Looking at Charles. "Imagine if I showed up at Duke Lorenzo's wearing a dress like this."

Charles nods. "They'd think you were dressed by your grandmother."

"Ma'am, are you an expert on Renaissance fashion?"

Renee considers her answer. "In a manner of speaking." Maxwell raises an eyebrow. "All right. Don't believe me. But you must have paintings from the period on hand."

"Of course."

"Very good. Just compare them but be sure you start with those from the time of Lorenzo the Magnificent because later artists tended to mix them up." Indicating the brooch on the right shoulder. "You'll also notice that these were always worn over the heart, never on the right side."

Maxwell looks over the display then dials a number on his cell phone.

"Dexter. Where are we storing the early Renaissance paintings not on display? Unpack a few with women as subjects if you don't mind. I'll be down shortly." He concludes the call. "All right. Is there anything else?"

Renee looks around and focuses on the next dress.

"Oh, those shoes with that dress? What were you thinking?"

"Wrong time period?"

"No, just plain wrong. If it were me, I'd go with something pointier — with beads perhaps."

Maxwell nods. "Thank you for your input Ms.—"

"Fox." Renee reaches into the inside pocket of her jacket then hands him her card. "Renee Fox. That's my home address and phone number should you want to contact me."

Maxwell takes the card and holds it up. "Thank you again, Ms. Fox. We'll certainly take your comments to heart and let you know if we have any further questions."

"Good enough." She looks at Charles. "Lunch at the Tavern?"

"Absolutely!"

When she was a small child, Katerina von Sachsen's father took her up onto his horse and rode her around the lands he'd acquired over the years and told her that one day her sons would inherit control over them, provided, of course, that she married and had sons. Nearing sixty, Katerina looks back on that time with a strong sense of irony. Never having found a suitable match, someone who met with her father's and her approval — and as his only child, her father took her opinion very seriously (unlike many fathers with daughters) — she drifted into late adulthood and beyond alone and with no one to pass on her legacy.

Still, Katerina doesn't mind. She'd rather die alone than live with someone she despised and most of the suitors she entertained were far more concerned with her property than her person. She has a notable face, but as many point out, she looks too much like her father, a stern and severe man on all matters not concerning his daughter on whom he doted. The skin on her face is rough and pockmarked and her nose is rather large and bent in the middle. Still, she has a charming smile and blue eyes that sparkle when she's happy and, having been educated in Greek and Latin, Katerina can converse intelligently on a variety of topics.

Well beyond the age when anyone would consider her a

suitable match, Katerina spends the majority of her time upstairs, wandering around her chambers, reading volumes from her father's extensive library, or writing in her diary, all but completely shunning human contact. The only person who sees her on a regular basis is the servant who brings her meals. The remainder of the staff isn't sure they'd recognize her if they ever saw her.

One afternoon, while dozing in her sitting room, Katerina awakens to the most wonderful sound she has ever heard: an old Saxon tune, sung by what Katerina first imagines is an angel sent to guide her to heaven. She waits a moment then realizes the voice is coming from the yard outside. She goes to the window and looks down. Seated outside the servant's quarters is a small, dark-haired girl, maybe five or six years old. As Katerina watches, the girl rises and walks back and forth along the path singing. Katerina puts down her book and hurries out of her chambers and down the stairs. Halfway down she's met by the servant bringing her a midafternoon snack.

"Lady Katerina?" the servant says and is ignored.

Katerina descends to the bottom floor and hurries back toward the kitchen, closest to where she'd seen the child. She bursts in, taking the servants by complete surprise, and they freeze then bow as the name "Katerina" is whispered among them. Katerina goes to the window and looks out.

"She's gone! Perhaps she was an angel."

She moves around to the next set of windows.

"Aha!"

Katerina rushes out the back door and grabs the little girl by the arm, startling her.

"Come with me."

They head into the kitchen.

"Whose child is this?"

A hush falls across the servants and they look to a woman at the far end of the kitchen, who had been chopping vegetables, but now stands, frozen, with her cleaver raised and her eyes pinned on the girl. She sets aside the utensil and moves toward Katerina with her head bowed.

"She's mine, Lady Katerina. Was she disturbing you?"

Katerina emits a brief laugh. "Oh, quite the contrary." She lifts the frightened child up and sits her on the kitchen table. She immediately takes note of the child's brilliant green eyes. "I was not at all disturbed."

She pats the little girl's cheek. "Do you realize you have a very special gift?"

"I'm not sure, ma'am. What kind of gift."

"You sing like an angel." Katerina points to the girl's mother. "What's your name?"

"Isabella, ma'am. This is my daughter, Renee."

"Renee." Katerina pinches her cheek. "Is her father in my employee?"

"No, my Lady. His name was Gregor. He died just before Renee was born."

"No matter. Tell me, Renee, how would you like a job in my house?"

"A job, ma'am?"

"Yes, but a fun job." Katerina looks back to Isabella. "I would like this child to come to my chambers each day and sing for me."

"Sing, ma'am? What would you like her to sing?"

"Anything. Whatever she knows, whatever she can learn from among my father's manuscripts." Turning back to Renee. "Think you'd like that?"

"If it's all right with my mother."

Isabella moves to Renee's side. "Of course it's all right with me." Isabella bows. "Lady Katerina, it would be an honor for my daughter to entertain you."

Katerina leans in toward Renee. "Why don't you come up and I'll show you where I live."

From that point on, every day in the afternoon until evening, Renee reports to Katerina's chambers and sings for an hour or more. The remainder of the time she's there, Katerina talks about her family, teaches Renee to read Greek and Latin and permits Renee to read anything from her library.

Renee becomes Katerina's closest confidante and her conduit with the rest of the staff, accepting Katerina's meals, returning the used plates, and issuing orders to the staff on Katerina's behalf. As the staff changes over time, the servants come to recognize Renee more easily than Katerina.

One afternoon while she's singing to Katerina, Renee hears her make a loud gasp and a few moments later, Katerina's hand drops over the side of the chair.

"Lady Katerina?"

She goes to her and checks to find Katerina is not breathing and her eyes are partially closed and staring downward.

Renee leaves Katerina's chambers and descends to the servant's quarters. Her mother sees her and goes to her.

"Renee? Why aren't you with Lady Katerina?"

"I think she's dead."

Several servants ascend to Katerina's room to confirm that she is dead. They begin making burial arrangements while confusion grips the rest of the staff as they now wonder exactly what they're supposed to do, since their employer is out of the picture. Their talks are curtailed by the announcement by a servant that a contingent of noblemen is approaching quickly. The servants begin to panic, but Renee reassures them.

"See to their needs and tell them that Lady Katerina will greet them at suppertime."

"Lady Katerina?"

"Lady Katerina," Renee tells him.

The servants do as they're told. As dinner is being served, the nobles suddenly rise with a spirited cheer. The servants look to see Renee, dressed in Katerina's clothing and wearing her signet ring, entering the dining hall. She looks more regal than the actual Katerina had ever looked.

"Gentlemen we are honored by your presence." The men bow and pay their respects. "You may remain with us as long as need be and while you are here you will want for nothing. If there's anything you lack, let us know and we'll do our best to fulfill it." She moves toward the door then stops and turns back to the guests. "There is a custom in our family to leave our guests with a pleasant memory. If you'll indulge me, I'd like to sing a song for you."

She sings a traditional Saxon tune to the delight of her guests then ascends back up to Katerina's chambers. The next morning, after the nobles depart, Renee descends again to the servants' quarters. When she enters, all the servants turn toward her and bow.

"What are you doing?"

The lead servant speaks. "We await your orders, Lady Katerina."

She looks around at them in bewilderment. Then a smile comes to her face. "Lady Isabella?"

Her mother comes forward. "Yes, Lady Katerina?"

"Accompany me to our chambers, please."

"Of course, Lady Katerina." Isabella winks.

Renee addresses the servants. "Lady Isabella and I will dine at sundown. Other than that, you may spend your time however you choose, so long as it's productive."

The lead servant bows. "Yes, my Lady."

From that point on, the same routine is followed whenever guests arrive. Word begins to spread of the hospitality of Lady Katerina and of her custom of singing to her guests. As the years pass, the servants begin to notice that Katerina doesn't seem to age. Those who remember the original take this to be a sign that Renee was truly meant to take her place.

As he approaches his fourteenth summer, Karl, son of Hogart, of the tribe known as the Fuchsleute or "fox people" as they are called by the neighboring tribes, knows it will soon be time to set out on his ritual hunt. From the earliest times, when Kanute followed the fox to the land of plenty, as a boy reaches a certain age, he is sent into the woods to find and track a fox to some destination, gain its trust, then await guidance from it. After a few days, the boy returns with the fox and can then be considered a man.

"What if I'm unsuccessful?" Karl has asked those who've accomplished the task.

The older men in the tribe have advised him. "If you fail on your first attempt, you can try again for the next three years."

"And after that?"

"If you are still unsuccessful, it is deemed you no longer follow the fox and you'll be dismissed from the tribe."

Karl is anxious to prove his worth and has been quizzing others who've performed this ritual for their tips on how best to accomplish it.

Karl is the oldest of Hogart's offspring and the only child of Hogart's first bride, Freya. She was overtaken by the withering sickness not quite a year after giving birth to Karl and died several months after that. Hogart wasted no time in choosing another bride, who gave him two sons, and his third wife who is the mother of his daughter and youngest son. The girl, though not quite nine, is already betrothed to the son of Hogart's trusted advisor. They will be married as soon as she reaches the proper age.

Karl has yet to be matched with someone as all are awaiting the outcome of his ritual hunt. Taller than average, with dark hair that he keeps just above shoulder length, the general wisdom is that he'll be successful in his first attempt.

His father has often remarked: "You are fleet of foot and a fine hunter. You'll do well, I suspect."

Karl's youngest brother, Gerd, is as anxious, if not more so than Karl for the ritual to begin. Gerd entertains notions of Karl taking him along and showing him techniques on how to be a good hunter.

Karl finally has to pull Gerd aside. "This is a trial I must face on my own. Your time will come soon enough."

Gerd is relentless, though and on the day Karl sets out on his quest, Gerd follows him, walking at a slower pace and after waiting until the shadow of the tree line reaches a particular spot to give Karl enough time to get well ahead of him. Karl left a trail which Gerd finds easy to follow and for several hours, Gerd stays right behind his older brother.

At last, he comes to a point where a second set of tracks start, and Gerd recognizes them as being those of a fox. Gerd can tell by the spacing in the tracks that the fox was running, and Karl had run after it. Gerd follows both sets until he comes to the edge of a ravine. The dirt around the edge is disturbed and a frightening thought overtakes Gerd as he slowly approaches the edge and looks down. His worse fears come true as he sees Karl lying at the bottom. Blood drips from a cut on his forehead and he doesn't appear to be breathing.

Gerd first thinks about running back to the tribe to get help, but then he decides to find a way down to Karl. If his brother is only slightly injured, Karl might still be able to complete his quest. Gerd searches along the ridge and finds a place where he can make it down into the ravine and he works his way to where Karl lies.

Approaching him, Gerd sees that Karl is not breathing, and his eyes are slightly open. Trying to keep his wits about him, Gerd looks around for a place to ascend the ravine so he can summon others from the tribe, but he can't find anyplace and doesn't feel confident about going back up the way he came down. He kneels beside his brother and begins to cry.

Suddenly, Karl's body jerks and his hands start shaking. Gerd jumps up and moves away, watching in amazement as the cut on Karl's head starts to heal. Karl opens his eyes and takes a deep breath, then sits up and looks around.

"What happened?" He turns toward Gerd who stares at him in amazement and can't speak. "What happened? Why are you looking at me like that?"

"You — you were dead. You weren't breathing then suddenly you were."

"That's not possible."

"It happened! I saw it myself. Your forehead was cut, but now it's not."

Karl brushes his hand over his forehead and notes the blood then looks around at the disturbed earth around him.

"I must have had the wind knocked out of me. I couldn't have been dead; otherwise how could I be talking to you now?"

Gerd helps Karl get up. Karl rubs his neck and right

rib cage.

"I am somewhat sore but that's probably a result of the fall." He crouches down to look Gerd in the eye and wags his finger at his brother. "This should serve as a lesson. This is no place for a child to be wandering around alone. Hop on my back and I'll carry you up then you should head back to the tribe."

He carries Gerd back up the side of the ravine using the accessible point Gerd discovered. Karl walks him halfway back to the tribe's location then stoops down.

"The tribe is straight that way. You should hurry because it will be dark soon." Gerd nods and starts away. "Oh. And not one word to anyone about this dying nonsense. No need in worrying anyone needlessly."

"Okay, I won't tell."

He heads back to the tribe and keeps his promise to Karl. Several days go by when suddenly a cheer arises from within the tribe. Gerd runs out to see Karl emerging from the woods and running alongside him is a grey fox. He is greeted by the people of the tribe.

Gerd whispers to him, "I didn't tell anyone."

Karl winks at him and jostles his hair.

As is custom, the fox is allowed to remain in the camp for as long as it chooses, while Karl tends to its care. At last, it runs into the brush, where it disappears back into the forest. That evening, a council is held where Karl is presented with his own fox pelt to wear over his right shoulder, denoting a tribal leader, a role which Karl, as a son of the current chieftain, will one day assume.

In the celebration that follows, Karl is allowed to join the men as they sing of the exploits of the tribe. For him, this is the highlight of his being recognized as a man, as Karl has long enjoyed hearing and singing the songs his tribe uses to commemorate various events in their history. While he is only allowed to sing with the men now, he has been learning the songs since before he was Gerd's age.

For the better part of the nineteenth and twentieth centuries, whenever Renee and Charles were in New York, they were part of traveling variety shows with a heavy emphasis on travel. Renee estimated that by the turn of the twentieth century, they had seen every inch of the continent, including parts most citizens had not and most likely never would see. She and Charles had talked about buying property in Manhattan, so they'd have more of a home whenever they were in the States.

So, it came as no surprise to Charles when he received a telegram from Renee while he was in London: "Just bought the most charming loft space in Soho and can't wait for you to see it. Lots of storage downstairs."

This had been in 1975 and since that time, neither of them has spent more than a month's time continuously in the dwelling, mainly when they were storing away some of their possessions. When it became evident they weren't going to be making as much use of it as they initially thought, they hired a management firm to rent it out to short-term tenants, usually for a six months or less at a time.

In the spring of 2004, Renee notified the management company that she needed them to take it off the rental market and she moved in over the summer. She hired a general contractor to start renovations she and Charles had been discussing for decades and took a hands-on role in the demolition and design process.

Looking over the plans, she pointed to a wall. "Is that load bearing?"

"I don't know."

"Well, find out and if it's not, I want it gone. Or replaced with columns if it is."

"Yes ma'am."

By the time Charles arrives in late-Summer of 2005, it's a showplace to rival the most expensive designer spaces. The area from the front door all the way to the entrance of the kitchen, nearly 2,400 square feet, is open and flanked by several giant windows with a northern exposure. The flooring is cherry wood with a dark stain, and in the center is a set of steps leading up to the living quarters which are enclosed. The furniture has been arranged to create several stations throughout the space and toward the far end is a massive bar with several taps and a functional sink. Across from the living area is another balcony space that spans the entire wall and is accessible on one end by a narrow staircase and at the other by a spiral ramp.

"What did you think when you got your first peek at it?" Renee says as Charles surveys the place.

"Sure beats the hell out of those shotgun shacks we used to stay in out west."

"You've got that right. Take a look at this."

She begins a tap dance routine on the hardwood floor.

"That's great." Charles joins her. They tap around the room mimicking each other's steps and gestures.

He takes her hand and pulls her to him, and they tango from one end of the room to the other then switch to a waltz step.

"We'll have hours of fun here."

Renee laughs. "You haven't even seen the bedroom yet."

"Oh, believe me, we'll get to that. Show me the kitchen."

She takes his hand and leads him into a kitchen worthy of a large hotel with a marble floor and granite countertops. There is a large refrigerator with glass doors, an industrial sized oven, and a large island with stools around one end. There's a sink along one wall and another in the middle of the island.

"We can entertain the troops here."

She punches him in the arm. "The lovely thing about this design is that we can eat over in the corner there by the window and it's nice and cozy, or we can open the dividers here and use the counter as a buffet for more formal dinners. In fact, I had one of those television chefs in the other night and he said his restaurant wasn't this well-equipped."

"Which one?"

"I'm blanking on his name. The one who grills."

"Ah, yes. I like that show. Very impressive." Charles gives her a quick kiss. "I'm thinking it's time to check out the bedroom."

"Gladly."

She takes his hand and pulls him toward the stairs.

Over the course of three centuries, visitors to the home of Katerina von Sachsen are steady but spaced out enough so as not to be overwhelming or to catch on that the woman who welcomes them hasn't changed much. It is almost a well-kept secret among certain travelers. With Charlemagne's victory over the Saxons and incorporation of Saxony into the Frankish empire, the occasional trickle of visitors becomes a flood and as soon as a few of these travelers discover Katerina's hospitality, more soon follow. As word of the Lady Katerina spreads, stories of her beauty and custom of singing to her visitors attracts the attention of countless suitors who arrive, hoping for the hand of the beautiful and talented noblewoman.

Katerina appoints a contingent of male servants to act as a buffer between her and the suitors, but as each day passes, more arrive with gifts, tributes, assorted trifles, and some of the worst poetry Katerina has ever heard. The most comical of it she posts on a wall near the servants' quarters so the literate among them can have a good laugh before turning in at night. Each evening, men serenade her from below the window she's led them to believe is hers. In truth, it's where the servants sort the laundry, but every now and then, in response to another impromptu concert, they'll clap, or coo, or make a noise similar to what one makes when one swoons to keep up the deception. Katerina's apparent lack of concern for the suitors does little to curtail the activity and she's at a complete loss for a way to relieve herself of the attention.

One afternoon a young man arrives, dressed in a very austere manner. As he's neither singing, nor reciting poetry, Katerina concludes that he's there for something other than her hand. She asks the servants to bring him to her private sitting room.

He is of average height, a bit dumpy but not terribly fat, with slumped shoulders and a slight limp. He's clean shaven and his hair is short. He's wearing a brown robe, tied at his waist by a cord and he's carrying a book which Katerina recognizes as a Latin Vulgate Bible. He introduces himself as Father Stephen.

"What brings you to our part of the world, Father?"

"I'm here to spread the good news, and to win souls for our savior."

"My guess is that having Charlemagne around makes your journeys in this territory much easier."

"My Lady is remarkably well informed on events of the day. Emperor Charlemagne only secured control of Saxony within the past decade."

"You hear a lot with people dropping in every few days. Events like that set a lot of tongues wagging."

Father Stephen presses his hands together and nods in acknowledgment. "Still, I'd be here even if Charlemagne wasn't in control. My mission is an act of faith, and it's through faith that all things are possible."

"Yes, I suppose that's one way to look at it. Still, from what I know of the martyrs, they seem to be the ones laying down their lives while the immortal entity they serve sits back watching the whole business in silence."

"I assure you, my Lady, their reward is a thousand-fold greater than the sacrifices they make."

Katerina rises and moves toward the window. Outside, a dozen men are jostling one another for a position closest to the laundry room window. Katerina gives a weary sigh and shakes her head.

"Your church, you're the one who has the nunneries, right? No men there."

"That is correct." Father Stephen slides toward the edge of his seat. "Have you entertained thoughts of joining the cloister?"

"Not at all. I assure you I'm cloistered enough up here." She waves her hand toward the window. "With these idiots running around day and night, I'm more so than usual." She moves away from the window and seems briefly lost in thought.

"You are welcome here, Father. Stay as long as you need, and I'll provide you with transportation and an escort."

"I am very much appreciative, my Lady. I look forward to familiarizing myself with your library and getting to know you better."

Each day when he's finished with his travels, they meet for a philosophical discourse. Though Katerina has little interest in religion, she welcomes the presence of someone with more experience of the world and a different opinion than hers. For his part, Father Stephen is greatly impressed with her command of Latin and Greek and her generosity in sharing volumes from her library.

After spending several weeks with him, Katerina feels she can trust Father Stephen enough to tell him about her lifespan as well as make him an offer.

"What is it you'd like to accomplish here, Father? And by here, I mean all over, not here in this room."

"My ultimate goal would be to erect a church to the glory of our Lord, but I sense it's a goal to be completed by one of my successors. Still, if I can lay the groundwork—"

Katerina cuts him off. "Father, what would you say if I told you that I'm prepared to give you a plot of land not far from here to build your church and all the resources you need to make it the finest in all of Christendom. Would that make you happy?"

Father Stephen stares at her in amazement. "My Lady, I'm at a loss for words. That would be a great blessing."

"Well don't go thanking god too quickly. There are some things you must do first."

"I'll do whatever's in my power."

Katerina pitches her head toward the sideboard. "On that table, you'll find a knife and some apples. Take the knife and one of the apples and slice it in half."

The priest does as he's instructed.

"Would you agree that the knife is sharp?"

"Yes, my Lady, very much so."

Lady Katerina loosens the top of her dress and exposes her right shoulder and the top of her arm. "I want you to take the knife and cut me." Tracing a line across her arm. "Right here."

Father Stephen looks shocked. "Lady Katerina, this is most unusual. I could never do that to you."

"Do you want your church or not? Think about it, Father. You could be the first man who Christianizes an entire region of Saxony. You could make Bishop, maybe even Pope."

"My Lady, I don't understand why you're asking this of me. Is this a test?"

"Not at all. There will be no consequences for this action. But if you fail to do as I ask, I'll send you on your way with a few coins and nothing more to show for this endeavor."

He contemplates this a few moments then looks back toward her with a concerned look. "Explain again what you want?"

"Cut me." She indicates the place again. "Do it now."

Without further hesitation, Father Stephen places the knife against her arm and presses down as he draws it across. She grits her teeth and grimaces but does not cry out as blood spills from the cut. Father Stephen starts to bow his head.

"Don't look away. Watch."

As Father Stephen watches, the cut stops bleeding and starts to heal itself. Within a few minutes, with the exception of a little redness and some residual blood, the area of the cut is completely healed.

Father Stephen is shocked. "It's a miracle! A true miracle."

"No, it isn't." Katerina readjusts her clothing. "It's just the way I am. Something I discovered I could do a long time ago. That's why I need your help and in exchange, I'll give you your church."

"I don't understand."

She spreads her arms before her. "If you had to guess at my age, how old would you say I am?"

He examines her, then scratches his head. "You're obviously rather young. I'd say no more than twenty-three or four."

"What if I told you I'm nearly three hundred years old?"

"That can't be. No one lives that long."

"No one heals as fast as I just did either. Ask the oldest

of the servants how long they've known me, and they'll confirm that they came to work for me when they were young and now they're not, but I still am — and that's the way it has been for generations." She waves dismissively. "It doesn't matter if you believe me or not. I still need your help and that's the second thing you must do if you want your church."

"What's that? I hope it doesn't involve anymore cutting."

"No, we're done with that. Look out this window. What do you see?"

He looks. "Numerous men seeking your hand."

"Right. Well, I'm not ready to give it away. And if I was, none of this bunch remotely interests me. They hound my servants day and night. Stand outside my windows professing their love." She snarls. "Writing odes. I can't take it anymore."

"How can I help?"

"I want you to help me come up with a reason why I'm not available to any of them. Why I'll never be available to them."

"Oh dear. That might be difficult."

"What I'm offering in exchange isn't small. I didn't expect it to be easy." She sits. "Now understand, I'm not asking that I be made permanently unavailable because someday someone might come along who interests me. I just need a good story that will make these men go away."

They ponder this quandary for many days and at last, Father Stephen descends to the main floor and asks that the suitors assemble in the banquet hall for an important announcement about Lady Katerina's choice for her hand.

Once all are assembled, Father Stephen gives a short oratory on the sanctity of marriage then says, "Lady Katerina has promised her hand to Bartolomeo of San Lucia."

The suitors exchange curious glances, and one yells out, "Who is Bartolomeo of San Lucia?"

Father Stephen pauses, thinking how best to phrase his response. "Do you not recognize the name of the great warrior king who's currently out fighting the infidels?"

En masse the suitors say, "Ah!" and among them can be heard, "Yes, the warrior king" and "infidels," as they nod their heads.

Father Stephen finishes. "My Lady has asked me to convey to you that she has taken a vow of chastity until her true love returns."

A groan goes up throughout the crowd and several suitors leave immediately. Of the few who stay, one says, "I suppose it's not worth staying around to see if she changes her mind?"

"Not at all," Father Stephen says. "Her choice is final, and she intends to spend her days in prayer for the safe return of Bartolomeo."

The remaining suitors shake their heads and depart. Once they're gone, Katerina calls Father Stephen back to her chambers. She's seated when he enters. "Good work, Father."

"I'm glad I could be of service." He gives a slight bow.

"Now the only question left is, where you would like your church?"

As the Fuchsleute continue their advancement out of the wilderness and into more settled areas, they find themselves clashing with legions of warriors equipped with body armor, swords, and knifes, crafted from a stronger type of metal than that employed by Hogart's people. It is learned that these forces are from a place called Rome and claim sovereignty over these lands. Hearing it, Hogart challenges his people to bring back as many of the fine weapons wielded by the Romans as they can carry after teaching them who has true sovereignty over the land. As his oldest son, Karl makes it his mission to engage as many of these troops as he can.

One afternoon, while on an outing with a group from his tribe, Karl hears the distinctive sound of marching and he knows it can only be the Romans. He climbs a ridge and sees a large encampment with men constantly marching in and out. His group will be greatly outnumbered if they attack on their own. Then an idea seizes Karl.

"Mareval, Lars, take some men and go into the other tribes. Tell them we're attacking the Romans and need their support."

"Do you think they'll agree?" Mareval says. "The Romans are a mighty army."

"If we strike as a unified force, they'll be outnumbered." Karl surveys the area. "There aren't many of them and if we hit them all at once, they'll be in disarray."

"What's their incentive to help?" Lars says.

"When the battle is done, we can divide the spoils or fight it out amongst ourselves to determine who gets everything."

The men agree and head out.

Lars and Mareval return with word that many of the other tribes agree and suggest that they launch their attack from the thickest part of the forest, so the Romans will have nowhere to hide.

"I doubt they'll hide," Karl says. "As you have observed, they're a very disciplined fighting force. But I'm in favor."

At the appointed time, the first of the tribes rush out of the woods, screaming and swinging axes, clubs, and spears as they meet the first of the legion. The other tribes follow suit and soon all of them are engaged. Karl finds himself in the thick of the fighting and he soon finds a focus for his fury. Amid the warriors on the ground is a commanding officer who looks to be only slightly older than Karl. He is riding a horse and using it to rally his men and to dart back and forth along the line of battle.

Karl swears an oath to himself: "Before this battle ends, I'll be riding that horse."

As he makes his way through the scene of battle, he notes that the officer on horseback looks different than the men fighting. His hair and skin are lighter, and he seems better nourished.

This causes Karl to wonder how many of the troops are Roman.

It makes more sense that a true Roman would be in a position of authority.

Karl has little time to consider it, though, as suddenly, the horse rears back, dropping the officer onto the ground. Rather than being stunned, he draws his sword and begins aggressively working his way through the carnage.

Karl rushes toward him, cuts him off, and challenges him. The Roman laughs and begins attacking Karl, who's swift on his feet and well skilled with his spear. On occasion, the Roman speaks to Karl, but Karl can't understand the language he's using. They fight for nearly half an hour before Karl finds himself knocked off balance, giving the Roman the opportunity to rush him and slash him across the midsection. Karl drops his staff and falls to his knees. He feels himself losing consciousness, but just before all goes dark, he sees several tribesmen surround and stab the Roman, who falls a few feet from Karl. Then Karl drops into complete darkness.

Karl opens his eyes, not knowing how long he's been there and not immediately remembering what happened. All around him are dead bodies, Roman forces, and members of many different tribes. Karl cannot see any of his people in the immediate vicinity.

He rolls to his back and sits up and the first thing that catches his eye is the Roman with whom he'd fought, only he isn't lying where Karl saw him fall. He's standing several yards away examining the battlefield. As Karl watches in bewilderment, the Roman turns and, seeing Karl, stares in disbelief for a few seconds. Then he heads toward Karl, carrying his sword. Karl quickly looks around for something to use in his defense, but as he does, the Roman stops, looks at the sword in his hand, and returns it to its sheath then continues to where Karl sits.

The Roman looks down at Karl with a half-smile then extends his hand to help him up. Karl is suspicious until the Roman holds up both hands, showing he has no weapon. Cautiously, Karl takes the Roman's hand and is pulled to his feet.

The Roman continues to look him over, shaking his head. Then he points to Karl's shirt, motioning for him to lift it. Karl does so and looks down to see a nasty scar across his midsection where he was cut. The Roman examines it closely then leans back and laughs heartily. He claps Karl on the shoulders and says what sounds to Karl like, "Morey dury day saltum."

The Roman removes a large leather pouch, takes Karl's hand, and places the pouch into it. Laughing, the Roman turns and walks away from Karl, leaving him to wonder what just happened. Karl checks the pouch to find it full of Roman coins. He stashes it under his clothes then heads off to find his tribe. Along the way, he collects several knives and swords, as well as a breastplate he's sure will fit him.

It will be many years before he finds his people.

Charles is walking along Fifth Avenue one afternoon when he spots a woman with short, dark hair, and a dancer's physique power walking toward him.

"Excuse me, Miss." He walks backwards a step to two beside her then turns and falls into step with her. "I'm certain we've met before."

She pauses. "Not the first time I've heard that today." Her accent sounds Californian. She gives him a close look. "But yes. You do look familiar."

He runs over several events in his head then raises a finger. "Ah!" He bows slightly. "Êtes-vous resté un danseur, Mlle?"

A wide grin crosses her face. "Oui, mais pas pour le travail."

"I knew it." Fox snaps his fingers. "Cotton States Exposition, Atlanta, Georgia, 1895, right?"

"Yes. Brigitte Marcal."

"Charles Fox. My wife and I were with the acting troupe from London."

Brigette nods emphatically. "I remember. Carlton and Carlotta. Though, I knew your wife as Renee if I recall correctly."

"You do indeed."

"So, is Renee also still around?"

"Yes, and here in New York. If you have a few minutes, I'll get her on the phone."

"Sure."

Charles dials Renee.

"Hi, Charlie."

"Remember the Cotton States Exposition in Atlanta?"

"The festival we attended in the 1890s?"

"Yeah, that's the one. Remember we hung out with the du Monde dance troupe?"

"Yes. Lively bunch."

"Do you recall the dancer, Brigitte?"

"Dark hair. Seemed to be able to hold her liquor."

"That's her. Guess who's standing not two feet away from me."

"You're kidding. I had no idea she was one of us."

"Neither did I."

"Well, let me speak to her."

"Oh, sure."

He hands Brigitte the phone.

"Renee?" In response to whatever Renee says, Brigitte responds in French. They converse in French for a few minutes then Brigitte says, "Tonight? Sorry. I have plans. I'm free tomorrow, though, if that works. Okay, great!" To Charles, "Do you—"

"No, no." He waves away the phone. Brigitte finishes the call and hands it back to him.

"I haven't had a conversation in French in ages."

"How long have you been in the States?"

"Los Angeles since the early twenties and New York for the past five years. In between I spent the last twenty years working my way across the country."

"So, you say you're not dancing professionally anymore. What are you doing?"

She extends her arms and twirls around. "I'm a fitness instructor."

"That would have been my next guess. So, I guess I'll be seeing you tomorrow. Did Renee give you directions?"

"She did and I'll be there. Oh, and thanks for being observant."

Charles winks. "The pleasure was all mine."

Katerina honors her promise to Father Stephen and finances a church that soon becomes one of the busiest in all of Saxony. The chapel isn't terribly large, accommodating up to two hundred people and the surrounding structures house a nunnery, a friary, and a monastery which finances itself by producing several types of beer, which the monks sell to weary travelers. Father Stephen oversees all aspects of the community, ministering to his flock, delivering the "good news" and watching as his little church grows and gains standing.

At last, word reaches him that he's been appointed a bishop and must return to Rome as soon as he's gotten his successor settled in. A few days following this news, a young man with dirty blond hair and an affable expression shows up announcing that he's Father Peter, the new priest appointed to the parish.

As their time together draws to a close, Katerina spends as much time with Father Stephen as she can. She's curious as to how his successor will handle her and her special circumstances.

"What did you tell Father Peter about me?"

"The only thing I could come up with which adequately explains your situation was that you are the daughter of Jesus and Mary Magdalene and that you carry the bloodline of Christ."

"You told him I carry the bloodline of Christ?"

"Well, first I had to convince him that Jesus and Mary Magdalene were married. Some branches of the Church consider that heresy."

"And he believed you?"

"Not at first. It took several lectures on faith to sway him. I'm not entirely sure he's convinced."

Katerina gives him a devilish smile. "I bet I can convince him."

Father Stephen stops. "Not the way you convinced me."

"Not at all. Something even more dramatic."

"I'm not sure I like the sound of that." Father Stephen resumes walking.

"You just bring him to me. I'll convince him."

Father Stephen arranges an audience with Katerina for

Peter. They talk around the topic of her lineage for more than half an hour, before tackling it. Father Peter is far from convinced.

"Father Peter, don't your scriptures say, 'Blessed are those who believe without seeing'?"

"That's true. Perhaps not that exact wording, but certainly the gist of it."

"Then since you don't believe you'll just have to see."

Saying this, she pulls a knife from her garments.

"Lady Katerina?" Father Stephen holds up his hand and takes a step toward her.

"No Father. He needs to see."

Before either priest can get to her, she places the knife below her ribcage and forces it upward, toward her heart. Both priests stop, horrified, staring at her as she removes then drops the knife. Blood pours from the wound and Katerina begins to sway.

"That really hurts." She speaks in a weak voice then coughs once bringing up blood. She collapses onto the floor, her eyes staring blankly ahead of her.

Fathers Stephen and Peter rush to her side.

"Lady Katerina?" Father Peter presses his ear to her chest then looks up at Father Stephen and shakes his head.

Father Stephen takes a mirror and holds it up to her mouth.

"No breath."

They rise then Father Peter picks up Katerina and takes her to the day bed and lays her on it. He closes her eyes then folds her hands across her midsection then rejoins Father Stephen on the other side of the room.

"What should we do?" Father Peter is terribly shaken by what he's just seen.

Father Stephen thinks it over for a moment. "Pray for guidance."

Father Peter nods and they kneel and lower their heads then make the sign of the cross. They pray silently.

While his eyes are closed, Father Stephen imagines that he hears a rustling noise from where Katerina lays, but he does not interrupt his prayers to look. Finally, he and Father Peter finish and look up and both are shocked to see Katerina's body missing. They rush over to the day bed, looking above and below it. Suddenly, from behind, Katerina's voice surprises them.

"Looking for me?"

They turn to see Katerina leaning against the wall, still wearing her bloody garments.

She finishes: "I probably should have waited for the morning of the third day but unlike my father, I'm a bit impatient."

Father Peter stares at her then sinks to his knees and folds his hands in front of him.

"My Lady! Forgive me for ever doubting you."

"Oh, that's all right." She goes to him and helps him to his feet. "I've dealt with my share of doubters in the past." She moves away from them. "You take Thomas. He doubted everything. If he wasn't standing right there when you rose from the dead, he'd ask for an encore — drove my father crazy."

Father Peter is beside himself. "My Lady, I can't believe you're actually here. I have so many questions. I don't know where to start."

Katerina turns back toward him and holds up her hand. "Now, you understand, there are some things I'm absolutely forbidden to discuss."

"Of course. But can you tell me, our Lord, what was he like as a man?"

Katerina thinks for a moment. "He was a very nice man, not nearly as austere as he's been portrayed in the Gospels. He always enjoyed a good joke."

"Really?" Father Peter is surprised.

Katerina glances at Father Stephen, who shakes his head and wipes his hand across his forehead then back along his hair.

"Oh yes. I can't remember a time when he wasn't laughing. Well, except when he was being crucified, that wasn't very funny. But other than that, a fun person to be around."

Katerina speaks to Father Peter for a few more minutes then goes to change her clothing as he excuses himself for his afternoon prayers. Once she's dressed, Father Stephen sits with Katerina shaking his head.

"You didn't tell me you could do that."

"I wasn't sure myself."

"You've never done that before?"

"No, but I figured with the long life, the healing, and everything else, I'd be okay. Very strange experience. I'm pretty sure I don't want to do that again."

"I hope not."

"Still, it's nice to know I can, just in case."

"I suppose." He returns to the topic they've been avoiding. "With this last barrier out of the way, there's nothing keeping me here now."

"I know." Katerina frowns. "It won't be the same with you gone."

"I must confess, it was always a regret of mine that I was never able to win you for our Lord." He smiles. "But something tells me you're going to be just fine."

She goes to him and gives him a long hug. "I could only hope that my actual father would have been as kind and giving as you've been. I will never forget you."

"I'll certainly never forget you."

With that, he leaves. Katerina watches from her window as he walks to the Rectory, and when he goes inside, she turns away, a single tear running down her cheek.

It has been many years since the battle that separated Karl der Füchse from his tribe, but he remains hopeful he'll one day be reunited with them. In the meantime, he's become a fine swordsman, using the weapons he took from the Romans, as well as more he's gathered along the way, to his advantage whenever threatened or challenged. He's also noted a decided lack of Romans over time, though whenever he encounters anything that looks like a legion, he generally avoids it.

He's never again seen the Roman officer who acted so strangely after the battle and Karl wonders if he was killed in another battle, died from old age, or perhaps is still alive. As he travels the land, Karl finds himself encountering more and more towns and villages and fewer roaming tribes. From the inhabitants he keeps up with the latest news and constantly asks about a particular tribe using a fox pelt as its standard.

One afternoon as he's making his way through a village, he finds himself confronted by two young men speaking a dialect he recognizes.

"Why are wearing that fox pelt on your shoulder?" one of the men says.

"I am Karl, son of Hogart of the Fuchsleute. It's my right to wear it."

"Hogart?" The two men speak together and exchange curious glances.

The first man says, "Hogart was chieftain when my father was a young man. He's been dead for more than thirty years."

"Thirty years?" Karl says, stunned by how much time has passed. "That can't be."

"It is," the second man says. "My father has told me stories of the exploits of our tribe under Hogart."

"Who is your father?"

"Mareval, the son of Krausen."

"I know him! We were raised together. He was there when we attacked the Romans."

The men exchange confused looks once more. Karl looks at them then shakes his head. "Are any of Hogart's offspring still alive?"

The two men continue to regard him suspiciously then step away from him and confer a few seconds.

"Will you accompany us to our chieftain?" the second man says. "I believe he can answer your questions."

Karl nods and follows the men nearly half a mile to a small settlement beside a river. As they enter, people step out of their huts and watch them advance along the main thoroughfare. Karl notes that the older people are watching him intently, sometimes pointing and conferring with one another.

Toward the center of the settlement, they stop, and the first man says, "You will need to drop your weapons."

"I assure you I mean no one any harm."

"Maybe so, but if you wish to speak to our chieftain, you'll do as we ask."

Karl takes off his backpack which contains several swords then unhooks his belt which has several knives on it. Once he's unarmed, they proceed to a large hut not far from the center of the settlement. The men go inside and are there for several minutes. When they exit, they are followed by an old man with a long white bead, whose back is bowed, his face heavily wrinkled and creased, moving slowly and deliberately. Something about him reminds Karl of his father. The man stops a few feet away and examines Karl with an odd look on his face.

"I am Gerd, son of Hogart, leader of the Fuchsleute."

Karl stares at him, unable to speak at first. "Gerd, this can't be you. You're old."

Gerd looks around at those assembled. "These men tell me you're claiming to be my brother Karl. Who are you really?"

"Can't you tell? Don't you recognize me?"

"You could just as easily be his son or grandson. What can you tell me that only he and I will know?"

"I could tell you my mother's name, your mother's name. I can recite our lineage. I could tell you—" He stops then thinks for a second and snaps his fingers. "Perhaps you can answer one question for me."

"What's that?"

"Did you ever tell anyone what happened when I went on my ritual hunt? How you found me at the bottom of a ravine and claimed I was dead."

Gerd's eyes widen and tears begin to form. "I never told anyone. Not father, not my wife or children." He embraces Karl. "I don't know how, but it is you!"

"I don't understand it either."

"They told us you were killed while fighting the Romans."

"I may have been, but as you recall, that won't necessarily keep me down for long."

They laugh. Gerd invites him into his hut and instructs his men to retrieve Karl's bags. When Karl exits later, he is met by a small group who identify themselves as men

Karl knew when he was originally with the tribe. He looks around at them and guesses most of their names correctly, though he finds it difficult to reconcile their aged appearance from when he knew them.

A man with a bushy, grey beard approaches. "I'm Lars. You sent me, with two others, to gather the tribes for the attack on the Romans."

"I remember you well." Karl takes Lars's hand. "I must assume we didn't win that one, for when I recovered, there was no one from the tribe around. Once I had time to think about it, I wondered why no one removed my body from the field."

The men look around at one another and laugh. One who's identified himself as Mareval says, "There weren't many left at that point. And we were mostly concerned with not becoming dead bodies ourselves."

"What happened?"

"The Romans were caught off guard and were in confusion early in the battle," Lars says. "But their commanders managed to keep them assembled. Still, they took many casualties."

Mareval continues. "Just as we felt we had gained the upper hand, we were set upon by another legion, coming to replace the first."

Lars takes up the tale. "Seems we caught them just as they were changing guards."

Another man adds, "Yes. Rather than crushing a decimated force, we found ourselves locked in another vicious battle with fresh forces."

"Incredible," Karl says. "It seemed like such a good plan."

"It was," Mareval says. "A good plan but executed at the wrong time. If we had struck a day before or after, the outcome may well have been very different."

"Still some good came of it," Lars continues. "We were forced to join with a few other tribes to survive and together we became a much stronger unit."

Karl stays with them for several weeks catching up and telling stories of his exploits since the battle. After a while, though he announces he must be going. Gerd protests.

"You should be with your tribe, my brother."

Karl disagrees. "It's not my tribe anymore. You've decided to anchor yourselves in this one place. I prefer to be mobile."

"Then take care of yourself, and remember, you always have a home here."

Karl nods then a thought crosses his mind. He reaches under his shirt and produces the leather pouch the Roman gave him. He takes out a single coin then hands it to Gerd.

"What's this?" Gerd examines it.

"It's a Roman coin. An officer at the battle where we were separated gave me this pouch full of them."

"Why?"

"I have no idea but having them has helped me out of a few jams in the past. Hang on to it and maybe it will bring you some luck."

Gerd nods. "I'll do just that."

With that, Karl leaves his people for the final time.

At the Fox's loft, Renee, Charles, and Brigitte catch up on old times.

"Weren't you working with Dennert at some point," Charles says.

Brigitte rolls her eyes. "If you want to call it that."

Renee laughs. "If you ask me, that aspect of the job would be much tougher work than learning the dance moves." She indicates Charles. "Makes me very glad we were a team."

"He was not a man you wanted angry with you. When I walked out on him, he blacklisted me throughout Paris and a good portion of France and England as well. Don't even ask what sort of places I ended up dancing in after that." She laughs. "All because of those damned cufflinks."

"Cufflinks?" Renee says.

"One evening when we were leaving the theater some woman stole a set of cufflinks from him that he'd purchased that day. He was so mad when he found out, he got a little rough with me and I had to rather forceful-ly remind him that wasn't part of our bargain. I left the next day and Dennert told everyone that if they wanted to continue to deal with him, they wouldn't give me the time of day."

"Typical," Renee says. "But it did eventually lead to your getting with du Monde."

"Eventually. Sort of like a stream of water eventually carving out the Grand Canyon."

"Say, Brigitte," Charles says, "when you were with du Monde in Paris, did you know Gisele Bourgeois?"

"I met her once, but I replaced her, so I never had the opportunity to dance with her. I've heard she was incred-ible."

"She was stunning," Renee says, "athletic but graceful — very unusual for the time."

"Tragic, tragic story," Charles says.

"I met her when she came by to welcome the group home. She had already lost a lot of weight and couldn't stop coughing. No one wanted to get too close to her. She was still very beautiful, though, even ravaged by the ill-ness."

"She was one of the most beautiful dancers I've ever seen," Renee says. "Present company excepted, of course."

Brigitte waves her hand at Renee. "For me, dance was always a means to an end. I'm told Gisele lived for it, though. I'm sorry I never got to work with her."

"Her work was dazzling," Charles says. "When she was onstage, no one could look away. She commanded every-one's attention."

Brigitte looks at the floor for a few seconds. "We were on our tour of America when we received a telegram from her brother that she had died. Everyone was really bro-ken up. At every subsequent performance, we began with a moment of silence, while the director held a candle. I always thought they were hypocrites, particularly the director. When Gisele really needed them they weren't there for her. One or two wanted to visit her but the di-rector wouldn't let them."

"But you spoke to her," Renee says.

"I don't like being told what to do. Even by someone who could send me packing." She takes a sip of her wine. "As I recall, some of the dancers were talking about the telegram and said that Gisele had a friend with her the last few months and who was there when she died."

Charles gives Renee a quick glance. "That was a friend of ours named Victoria. She's a long-timer as well."

"Victoria?" Brigitte says. "Do you know if she came to America?"

Charles and Renee look at one another and Charles says, "She did. Why do you ask?"

"There's this major philanthropist in town, named Victoria Wells," Brigitte says. "I've always suspected that she's one of us."

"What makes you think that?" Renee asks.

"She's really young, but there's been someone using that name in New York for most of the last century. One of my clients is a broker on Wall Street and I heard from him that the rumor is that the original Victoria Wells was a little kooky and left her entire fortune to a great grand-niece but only on the condition that she change her name to Victoria Wells."

She leans in. "But I did some digging, and the niece story doesn't hold water. If someone named Victoria Wells ever left a will in New York, I can't any find record of it. Oh, and I've heard that she has this nasty scar on her neck which she never talks about. Whenever the subject comes up she says it's a part of her life she's put behind her."

"A scar?" Charles asks. "Like someone cut her throat at some point?"

"That's what I've heard," Brigitte says. "The kind of cut the average person doesn't wake up from."

Charles exchanges a knowing glance with Renee. "That's our Victoria."

"So, Victoria was with Gisele when she died?"

"She was," Renee says. "She was by Gisele's side night and day for months. When Gisele's brother was finally able to get to her, he found them together. Gisele had been dead for who knows how long."

"She must have been devastated," Brigitte says.

"She was," Charles says. "They met in Paris in 1890 and they were virtually inseparable until Gisele began to prepare for the continental tour. We had just gotten back to England when we heard about Gisele's death and just barely got there in time for the funeral."

"Their relationship was scandalous actually," Renee says with a light tone. "They were very open about it."

"We heard that the priest at the family's church at first refused to let her be buried in the family plot in the churchyard," Charles says. "He used the old saw about her illness being god's judgment."

"Where do they get this stuff?" Brigitte says, shaking her head.

"He changed his mind soon after though," Renee adds. "No one was ever sure why."

Charles leans toward Brigitte and says, "So, how would we go about finding this Victoria Wells?"

"She owns a recording company but spends most of her time at this charity she founded, Caring Hands, Loving Hearts."

Charles and Renee look at one another and wink.

Since leaving his people, Karl has been wandering the land for many years. He visits a town or village to keep up with what's happening in the region, but otherwise, he spends his time on the road, interacting with others who, like him, aren't quite ready to end their nomadic lives. Finally, he comes to a small hamlet in an isolated region which Karl suspects is controlled by the Visigoths. Entering the town, he finds the people hard at work, so busy that most give him little notice as he walks along the main roadway. He comes to an odd structure near the center of town, a building with a high spire on it and a cross at the top. Karl stares at it a moment then signals to a man walking nearby.

"What sort of building is this?"

The man looks at him then at the building. "It's a church. The last group who came through with troops

and weapons told us to build it and said we're now all
Christians."

Karl nods. "That's why I keep moving. They can't convert you if they can't catch you." He looks around. "What
town am I in?"

"It's no town. It's part of the holdings of our master,
Ortin."

"Why do you call him master?"

"Because the last few who didn't were run through by
his sword. The rest of us decided to err on the side of not
getting run through by a sword."

"I see." Karl nods to the man. "Thanks for the information. Good day to you."

He continues to stroll around the grounds until he
hears hoof beats approaching and turns to see a large,
well-dressed man entering the square riding a dark horse
with white markings. As he advances, people stop whatever they're doing and kneel. Before long, Karl realizes
he's the only one not kneeling. The man on horseback
rides to him and addresses him angrily.

"Bow before your master, churl. Or you'll pay the price
for your insolence."

Karl looks him in the eye and speaks loudly and calmly.
"You must be Ortin."

"I am."

"Then know this, Ortin: I am Karl, son of Hogart, and
I bow to no man."

A murmur goes through those around the square.

Ortin turns to a pair of young men kneeling nearby.
"Take my horse."

"Yes, Master Ortin." One of the young men walks over
to take the reins of the horse. Ortin hops off and pulls his
sword.

"I don't care what you call yourself. Bow before your
master."

Karl unhooks his pack then removes a sword from it
and lets the pack drop.

"And I repeat, I bow to no man."

"Then you shall serve as an example to the rest."

Ortin moves toward Karl, who raises his sword.

They make several passes, making contact a time or two, but largely testing one another. Ortin seems to know what he's doing, so Karl carefully plots a plan of attack. Finally, they engage, both fighting aggressively and neither able to gain a competitive advantage.

Ortin removes a knife and makes several slashes at Karl but misses him each time. Karl finally manages to disarm Ortin of the knife, but he continues to wield the sword forcefully. Finally, Karl connects with Ortin's forearm, causing him to toss his sword several feet away. In response, Ortin rushes back to his horse and grabs an axe, which he swings wildly as he advances on Karl a second time. Karl holds him off as well as he can, but at last, he loses his grip on his sword.

Ortin raises the axe to deliver a final blow, but Karl ducks down, sweeping one leg under Ortin and knocking him to the ground. Karl then dives toward the first weapon he sees, which is Ortin's sword. He hits the ground and rolls, grabbing the sword then getting to his feet in a crouched position. Ortin has recovered and rushes Karl with the axe held high above his head. Karl remains in position until Ortin is upon him then he brings the sword up forcefully, shoving it below Ortin's ribcage and thrusting upwards until the point comes out of Ortin's left shoulder. Ortin cries out then drops his axe and falls to the ground, dead.

Karl stands and looks down at him.

"Now you're an example."

Karl removes the sword and turns back toward the assembled townsfolk. They stare at him in disbelief, then all bow before him.

Karl walks toward them. The only one still standing is the one tending to Ortin's horse. He averts his eyes.

"What are you doing?" Noting that the man keeps his head down. "Look at me. Why are you acting like this?"

The young man faces Karl. "You have defeated Master Ortin in single combat. You are now our master."

"Seriously?" He looks around at the people. "Would everyone please stand up and look at me?"

The townsfolk do as they are told.

Karl returns to the young man.

"So, let me get this straight. Because I killed this guy, you all now work for me?"

"That's right. You now control his lands, his cattle, his servants, and his castle."

"He has a castle?"

"No, you have a castle. He had one."

"Can I see it?"

The young man gives him a curious look. "Aren't you forgetting something?"

"Forgetting what?"

A woman in the crowd calls out to Karl. "Aren't you going to chop off Ortin's head and put it on a pike which you can carry with you for all to see?"

"Why would I want to do that?"

Another person from the crowd calls out: "How else will people know you've defeated him?"

"Good point." Karl waves a finger at him. Karl turns to some of the men. "Bring me a large axe!"

The townfolk exchange confused looks and someone from the crowd shouts, "Why don't you just use Ortin's?"

Another says, "Yeah. I mean, the sword worked."

Karl looks, then points at the axe that's lying near Ortin. "Ahh! Never mind."

He retrieves the axe and instructs two men to place Ortin's body on a tree stump. With two quick whacks, Karl removes Ortin's head. As it drops to the ground, the people cheer.

"I take it Ortin wasn't very popular," Karl says to an old man standing nearby.

"He was okay if you liked vicious beatings and savage rape," the old man answers.

"Were there a lot of people who did?"

Another man puts a finger beside his nose. "You'd be surprised."

Some of the townspeople bring a tent pole that's turned upside down and Karl fits Ortin's head onto it snuggly.

"That should do it," Karl says. "Now let's see that castle. Can you point me in the right direction?"

"Take the main road two miles then turn left at the first

mulberry tree you find," the young man holding the horse says. "You can't miss the tree. It's right in front of this huge castle."

Karl starts to walk toward the edge of town holding the pike.

"Sir?" the man holding the horse says. "Don't you think it would be quicker to ride your horse?"

Karl looks back. "A horse? Oh, that horse."

He hands the pike to the young man then mounts the horse and retrieves the pike. Before he departs, he addresses the people. "From this day forth, it is no longer necessary to kneel before me. Just a quick nod or slight bow will do if you feel like it. And don't work so hard. Take a minute or two each day to appreciate the finer things."

Someone in the crowd calls out, "Like what?"

Karl considers it. "You'll think of something."

The people cheer as Karl takes off toward the castle. As he moves along, holding Ortin's head on the pike, people stop and stare, and those who realize whose head it is cheer and wave their arms around. Reaching the mulberry tree, Karl turns onto a long road that leads up to the castle. Arriving there, he's confronted by a man in the turret.

"We're not to receive visitors while our master Ortin is away."

"Your master Ortin came with me. A part of him at least."

The man gives him a curious look. "Hold it up where I can see it."

Karl does as he's instructed and suddenly the man gets an excited look on his face and begins jumping up and down. "Open the gates! Open the gates!"

Once he's safely inside and has explained himself to the guards surrounding the parapet, Karl requests that all the household staff assemble in the courtyard so he can address them. Among those assembled, he notes a young blonde woman standing near a muscular young man and they keep exchanging glances while trying desperately to look like they aren't.

"I am Karl der Füchse, and as you can see, I have killed Ortin in single combat, as evidenced by the fact that I chopped off his head and put it on this stick. I'm told that makes me your master."

Those assembled mumble in generally affirmative tones. The oldest of the servants steps forward. "You are quite correct sir."

"You will find me to be a tough, but fair master, and I'm not really all that tough. All I ask is that you do a good day's work and don't cause any major mischief. Otherwise, whatever you do is your business."

Those assembled smile and nod to one another.

"Now I'm hungry and would like some supper. Who takes care of that?"

The young blonde woman steps forward and curtseys.

"That would be me, sir."

Karl nods. "What's your name?"

"Susse."

"Then Susse, I'll see you when you bring my meal to my quarters." The girl, who seems overly anxious, hurries off.

Karl realizes he's still holding the pike and hands it off to a servant with instructions to, "Find someplace to prominently display this for all to see."

"Yes, sir!"

Karl turns back to the older servant. "And now, if some-one will be so kind to attend to my horse then show me to my quarters. So, I can be there when the food arrives."

"Right this way," the elder servant says.

"Oh, one more thing." Karl snaps his fingers and turns back to the staff. "Who here can paint? Pictures, I mean, not walls."

A boy in his late teens raises his hand.

"Can you make me a bold rendering of a fox? I want to replace that boar's head out front with it."

"I can, sir."

Karl gives him a thumbs up.

"What are you called?" Karl asks the older servant as they walk to Karl's quarters.

"Gareth, sir."

"Well Gareth, I shall be counting on you to give me the

lay of the land over the next few days."

"Certainly, sir. I'll do whatever you require."

They reach Karl's quarters. "Oh, if the sheets haven't been replaced from the last time Ortin was here, could you have someone see to that?"

"The sheets are replaced every morning, sir. Master Ortin never liked to lie on dirty linen."

Karl nods and enters his room. "Good enough — maybe every other day in my case — maybe every week. We'll figure that out, though. You may go, Gareth, but keep yourself available in case I have any other questions."

A while later, there's a knock at the door and Susse enters with a tray with meat and bread on it. Averting her eyes, she sets it on the small table near where Karl is sitting and bows. Then she goes to the foot of the bed and sits, her hands folded in front of her, head down.

"What are you doing?" Karl says.

"Master Ortin expected me to remain while he ate so he could have me afterward. I wasn't sure if you'd want the same."

"He did that?"

"Yes sir."

"You don't need to worry about that anymore. Also, I would prefer it if you look at me when addressing me. If you could maybe pass that around."

She looks up at him with a smile.

"Gladly, sir."

"Didn't I see you with a young man during the assembly?"

"Yes sir. He's Varn and he would be my intended, but master Ortin forbade us from marrying. He wanted me all to himself."

"Oh, he did, did he?" Karl rises and holds out his hand to her. "Come with me."

They exit and descend to the servant's quarters. Gareth sees them coming and rouses everyone else. Karl says to Susse, "Go get him."

She does as she's told.

Karl leans toward Gareth. "As master of the house, do I have the authority to marry people?"

"As master of the house you have the authority to do pretty much whatever you want, though it may need to be sanctioned by the church at some point. As far as the household servants are concerned, you essentially own us and can do with us whatever pleases you."

Karl shakes his head. "That won't do at all. Gareth let everyone know there are going to be some changes around here."

"Yes sir."

Susse returns with Varn. Karl asks for their hands and places them together.

"By the authority vested in me as head of this house and master of these lands, I declare you to be man and wife."

The servants' quarters erupt with cheers when the couple kisses one another.

Karl addresses the servants. "From this day forth, anyone who attempts to abuse any one of you within the confines of this house or elsewhere, will have to deal with me. Do you understand?"

The servants cheer again.

Charles and Renee stop in at the Manhattan location of Caring Hands, Loving Hearts and ask for Victoria.

"Who shall I say is here?"

"Tell her it's Carlton and Carlotta," Charles says to which Renee giggles.

The receptionist nods and dials Victoria's extension.

"Ms. Wells? You have some visitors. They said to tell you it's Carlton and Carlotta."

From the other end of the line, Charles and Renee hear an excited shriek which causes the receptionist to pull the earpiece out of her ear.

"Ms. Wells? She hung up."

From the side hallway, they hear the quick patter of feet on the tiles and a few seconds later, Victoria appears in the doorway grinning broadly. Seeing Charles and Renee, she covers her mouth and leans slightly forward then hops up and down clapping her hands.

"Oh my god!" She rushes over and leaps into Charles' arms. "Charlie!" He hands her off to Renee. Victoria gives her a bear hug and kisses her multiple times on the cheek. "How long has it been?"

Charles offers, "It seems like a century."

Victoria looks at him then the receptionist, and composes herself. "It does." She steps back and waves her hand toward the doorway where she entered. "Please, join me in my office. We have a lot of catching up to do. Merrill, hold all calls except Dana or an extreme emergency."

As they walk, Renee says in a low voice, "I must say you have perfected the art of hiding in plain sight. I've been in town for most of this year and hadn't even heard your name."

"And we hear you've established quite a name here," Charles says.

"You don't know the half of it." Victoria shows them into her office. "I have a record label, a major charity and one of the largest investment portfolios on the East Coast."

"Our little girl has grown up," Renee says, clapping her hands.

"Speaking of which, whatever happened to your evil uncle?" Charles inquires.

Victoria puts her hands up. "Please, we haven't seen each other in over a hundred years. Let's not start with dismal topics. Suffice it to say, he's not a danger to anyone currently."

"Fair enough," Charles says. "You look great."

"She must be in love," Renee says.

"Did I hear you mention the name Dana?" Charles says.

"Yes and you have to meet her. She is— I don't know how to even describe all she means to me— let's just say she's been there for me through thick and thin and we just love one another more all the time."

"Is she—" Renee asks.

Victoria shakes her head. "I don't think so, but when has that stopped me before?"

"That is something I've always admired about you," Charles says.

Renee continues, "You aren't afraid to face the numbers."

"Why pass up a chance to be with someone so special?" Victoria says.

They speak for more than an hour then Victoria invites them to her apartment.

"Unfortunately, we have plans for this evening," Renee says, "but we're having a party in a few days, and we expect you to be there."

"Bring Dana," Charles says. "I look forward to meeting the person who's made you this happy."

"You just try to keep us away," Victoria says.

Settling into his new home, Karl finds he has a lot of free time on his hands, so he sets out to learn as much as he can that will help him with his new responsibilities. Ortin's library isn't much more than a few thick, dusty tomes, with crosses embossed on the front, the spines of which have never been broken — a moot point since Karl can't read them. So, Karl hops on his horse one morning, bids farewell to the staff and promises to return within a few days, though he does encourage them to take a good look at him in case it's just his head that returns.

He pauses on the crest of a hill, overlooking a valley dotted by settlements. From this distance, all look pretty much the same and he has no idea where to start in his quest for knowledge. He recalls the precision and discipline of the Romans he and his tribe fought and reasons that people capable of fielding such an army must be very advanced. The only problem is, he doesn't know where to find any Romans any longer and isn't sure he'd even recognize one unless the individual is wearing body armor and carrying a sword.

His thoughts are interrupted by a disturbance not far from where he sits. Karl guides his horse toward the activity, which sounds like angry voices taunting someone. Karl comes into a clearing to find several young men surrounding an older man dressed in black and wearing a skullcap. A rope is around the older man's neck and the younger men have him standing on a makeshift ladder. Not far away is a large fire.

Karl rides into the clearing. "What's going on here? What has this man done to warrant this treatment?"

The apparent leader of the group comes forward. "He's a Jew."

Karl stares at him a moment then repeats himself more slowly. "What has he done to warrant this treatment?"

Another of the men yells out, "His kind killed our Lord."

A second man agrees then says, "And now he's contaminating our streams. Since he set up his shop in our village our cattle have gotten sick, and it has not rained for many months."

Karl looks around at them then addresses the accused. "Have you done all these things?"

"I have not. There was no rain for months before I arrived, and I've never gone near their cattle."

"By whose authority do you condemn this man?"

"By the authority of Master Ortin," the leader says. "He ordered us to round up any Jews we found within his lands."

Karl nods. "Cut him down."

The leader advances toward Karl holding a club.

"Who are you to tell us this?"

Karl swings a leg over the top of his horse and jumps to the ground and pulls out the sword he used to kill Ortin, which he points at the leader's throat. "I'm the man who'll end your life in a matter of seconds if you don't do as I say. Then I'll just cut him down myself."

The leader's eyes widen, and he begins to shake. He waves to his compatriots who cut the rope. The Jewish man climbs down and removes the rope from around his neck.

Karl proclaims: "Let it be known that there's a new decree. Ortin is dead. I killed him with his own sword." He holds up the sword. "If you don't believe me, stop by the castle and you can see his head." He pauses. "Late afternoon the lines are shorter — just a tip. All individuals on these lands are now under the protection of Karl der Füchse and anyone who raises a hand to one of these subjects for any reason will answer directly to me."

Once the gang has departed, the man says to Karl, "I am indebted to you. I was certain my life was done before you arrived."

"I'm just glad I could be of service. Who are you and what do you do?"

"I am Isaac ben Moises. I'm a scribe."

"A scribe. That means you read and write, correct?"

"That's correct. Greek and Latin, Hebrew, and Arabic."

"I'm going to assume you aren't currently employed."

"Despite your decree there are many who would gladly do me harm. It's doubtful I'll find many employers here."

Karl climbs back onto his horse then extends his hand. "You've just found one."

He helps Isaac up onto the back of his horse and they head back to the castle.

Once there, Karl outlines what he expects of Isaac, who listens, stroking his beard. When Karl is finished, Isaac says, "I can do all you've outlined without a problem." One item catches his eye. "You say you want me to also teach some of the servants to read and write."

"That's correct. Those who want to learn."

"Why would you want your servants to know Greek and Latin?"

"There may come a time when one of them will need to stand in for me in a transaction, and I want to ensure that whoever that is will know how to understand what he's agreeing to. Besides, what good does it do to have an education if there's no one else around who can hold a decent conversation?"

Isaac nods.

"Now as you can see, my library isn't much to speak of right now. Ortin apparently wasn't much of a reader, which was obvious the first and only time I met him, but that's beside the point." He walks toward the bookcases. "Where can I find the best literature money can buy?"

"What would you like? Plays, poetry, philosophic discourse, history?"

"Yes! And religious items as well, but no one religion."

Isaac considers this a moment. "I believe I can accommodate all of that. If you'll be so kind as to send some of your servants to seek out my friends, we can have a fair number of titles in a few weeks and the remainder of what you want within a matter of months."

"Excellent! Now, let's go meet the staff."

The servants are once again assembled in the courtyard. When Karl appears before them with Isaac a low murmur goes through the group.

"This is Isaac ben Moises, and as you can see, he's a Jew." Another murmur goes through the crowd. Karl speaks up quickly. "Now, just as I've sworn to protect each of you, I've also sworn to protect him, and others like him. Is that clear?"

The servants give generally agreeable responses.

"Isaac is very well educated. He can both read and write, and I have hired him to work in the household as a scribe. I have also asked him to teach me to read and write Latin and Greek. I also wish to extend this opportunity to any one of you who wishes to learn."

This time a more excited murmur goes through the crowd. One in back says, "Who can take part?"

"Anyone," Karl says. "Maybe a few at first, so Isaac's not overwhelmed, but if all of you want to learn, we'll find a way to accommodate you."

The servants look around and nod to one another. Susse and Varn step forward. Karl acknowledges them. Several others come forward and Isaac and Karl meet with them for a few minutes.

"Now hopefully this will make a good start," Karl says, "and once we have a few around who know what they're doing, they can begin teaching others."

He dismisses all but those who are talking to Isaac. Within a few months, the books Isaac promised start to arrive and by that time Karl and at least two of the servants have learned enough to make some sense out of them. As the library grows, so does the number of people in the household who can read the works.

Among the volumes are collections of Greek and Roman tragedies and comedies. Isaac suggests they use them to help with their conversational language and within a few weeks, Karl and several others know them well enough to recite them from memory. Karl suggests putting on a show for the rest of the household and the resulting performance is very well received.

One afternoon, a contingent of armed men arrives along with a man arrayed in the finest garments anyone has ever seen and wearing an ornate hat. As they ride up the path to the castle, they encounter two men in rustic clothing having a conversation in a language the leader of the armed men doesn't recognize. The man in the ornate hat gives them a curious look and addresses them in the same language. One of the men scratches his head and points toward the castle before continuing his conversation. The man in the hat nods and continues along the path.

"What language was that?" the leader of the warriors says.

"It's Latin," the man in the hat says.

"I didn't think that was spoken outside the church," the leader says.

The man in the hat shakes his head as they come to the entrance to the castle grounds. They announce themselves to the watch, who disappears without opening the gates then reappears a few minutes later to announce that the head of the household will greet the men shortly. Nearly five minutes later, a young man with dark hair appears atop one of the parapets.

"I'm Karl der Füchse. I'm told you wish to speak with me."

"Will you not invite us in, so we may speak like proper gentlemen?" the man with the ornate hat says.

"Most proper gentlemen don't have an armed escort. So, until I know your business, I'll leave you where you are."

The man with the ornate hat looks around at his contingent then back to Karl. "I am Bishop Francois, and I am here at the direction of the Pope. It has been rumored that you harbor Christ killers, and heretics, and that you have not allowed our messengers to deliver the news of our Lord to this region."

"If your messengers are the ones wearing the brown robes, on two occasions they threatened some of the townsfolk, and one was outwardly abusive. Such behavior is not tolerated in this region regardless of why the person is here. And if, by Christ killers, you mean Jews then yes, they live here unhindered. As for heretics, I'm not even sure what those are. If honoring one's native customs makes one a heretic, you've got quite a job ahead of you."

The Bishop looks around at the men with him as he considers what he's heard.

"You appear to have a very nice life here," the Bishop says. "But how do you think you would fare if we returned with a thousand dedicated warriors to press our cause?"

Karl stares at them a moment then nods to the watch who raises a horn to his lips and gives a sustained blow. Instantly, all along the walls of the castle, archers appear with their arrows pointed at the contingent. A rumbling is heard from all around, and from every wooded parcel of land troops begin streaming out into the fields surrounding the castle. This goes on for many minutes and when done, there are armed men assembled for as far as the eye can see in any direction, nearly five thousand in all. Karl looks around then back to the contingent.

"I think I'd manage."

The Bishop and his men look around them fearfully. Karl gives them a few moments to contemplate their situation.

"Send your men away Bishop, and you'll be welcomed as our guest. Then perhaps we can meet like proper gentlemen. I will personally guarantee your safety until you're back with your people. Otherwise, you may be on your way, and we'll not raise a hand against you."

The Bishop agrees and is admitted to the grounds. Several days later, he departs with an agreement on the part of Karl to support the building of a Christian cathedral provided that no one is converted who doesn't want to be and that the Jews in the region are left alone. His accord with the church settles a great deal of tension that had been building for a number of years and which had led to numerous monks and friars being sent to the region, sometimes with armed escorts, to Christianize the population.

With the sanction of the church, though not totally in agreement with it, Karl decides to sit back and let society change around him. Initially under the rule of the Visigoths, Karl receives news that a new group, the Franks, are now in command of the region he inhabits. A new king, who's being hailed as Charles the Great, or Charlemagne, occupies the throne and Karl decides that he should perhaps make an appearance at court. Taking his cue from Charlemagne, Karl adopts a Frankish version of his name, becoming Charles Renard.

Learning that Charlemagne has gone to Rome to receive the blessing of the Pope, Charles sets out for Rome himself, hoping for an audience with the king. It will also be his first time visiting the city which yielded so many of the soldiers he and his tribe fought long ago.

He finds it to be a fascinating city with wonderful architecture and a thriving community. As he's wandering around the church grounds, he spots a face he recognizes from many centuries earlier. He approaches the man cautiously, not sure if he's seeing who he thinks he sees but as he's a short way away from him the man glances in his direction and a look of recognition crosses his face. It's the Roman officer Charles fought just before being separated from his tribe.

Noting his clothing, the man speaks to him in Latin. "Nice to see you've improved your station."

Charles answers in Latin. "Bet you never imagined a sack of coins could go so far."

"And you've learned the vernacular. I got the impression you didn't fully appreciate what I told you at our last encounter."

"I didn't. What was it?"

"Morituri te salutant. It's what the gladiators said as they entered battle. I use it as a sort of taunt to the short-timers."

"Short-timers?"

"Those who don't live as long as we do."

Charles nods. "I'm Charles Renard."

"Still a fox person, I see. These days, I'm known as Bergeron."

"Bergeron?"

"Yes. I came up with a composite name once and people kept writing this instead. After a while, I stopped correcting them."

"If it works, it works. Speaking of the coins, why did you give them to me?"

"I thought you'd need them. It was doubtful you'd find your tribe. Whatever was left had undoubtedly scattered with all the others. You see, you had a very good plan, but the execution was poorly timed."

"That's what I've been told."

"In some ways, though, you were fortunate. The Romans you were facing were mercenaries. If that had been an actual Roman legion during the height of the Empire, not only would your people have been defeated that day, but we'd have pursued you and captured or killed the rest."

"What's that you said about timing?"

They walk a little way before Bergeron continues. "It seems your Frankish pretender will be crowned emperor before long."

"Emperor of Rome?

"By no means." Bergeron sounds indignant. "The buildings are Rome, but the people most certainly are not. They call it the Holy Roman Empire — an insult to any true Roman."

"Haven't they retained some of the trappings?"

"Mimicry. Like a parrot answering back what you've taught him to say without comprehending any of it. Take this whole nonsense of the emperor needing the sanction of the church. A true Roman emperor was the church, a god incarnate."

"You didn't really believe that did you?"

"I lived through the reigns of Tiberius, Caligula, Nero. If those were examples of gods, then heaven's none the better for it." He sighs. "But it was a necessary myth. The rabble needed someone to venerate or else they'd have been up in arms all the time. The army had enough problems abroad without having to deal with uprisings at home."

He pauses to look around at the architecture then indicates the Basilica. "That's where Charlemagne is to be crowned. He thinks he's only here to secure the Pope's blessing, but there's more to it than that."

"Does he know?"

"Of course, he knows. It's the worst kept secret in the western world; the only reason he's coming to Rome in fact."

"So why are you here?"

"Paying my respects. I have some landholdings in and around Constantinople and I'd like to keep them. I'm also hoping to stem the tide of Christian warriors they keep sending out to deliver the good news." He shakes his head. "If these fools knew all I know about their 'savior' they'd realize what a sham this all is."

"Really. Do tell."

"Perhaps another time. It gets rather complicated." Bergeron surveys the area and laughs. "Most of the conventions of the Church were coopted from Rome. The pantheon of gods became many of the initial saints; the vestal virgins became the nuns. Deification of the dead has been replaced by sainthood. I'd almost feel right at home if it weren't for all the crosses."

"What's that about? I'm led to believe the Christian symbol is the fish."

"Constantine." Bergeron speaks with a note of disgust in his voice. "He's the emperor on the coins I gave you. He claimed to have had a vision of a cross on the sun just before he won a significant battle and took that to be a sign from the Lord — hence, the cross."

They walk on a few more yards in silence.

"So, what exactly are we?"

Bergeron considers the question a moment. "We're people. We live longer. Why? Who knows?"

"Have you figured out how fast you're aging?"

"I'm guessing one year for every forty or fifty years for a regular person."

Charles processes this and nods. "That sounds about right. Have you run into others?"

"Once in a while. Of course, it's not like we wear our attribute on our sleeves. We look like average people to average people as well as to others like us. Given how spread out we can become, it's easy to go a long time without running into someone you've seen."

As they're speaking, a bishop approaches them. "Is one of you Bergeron?"

"I am."

"The Pope has asked me to speak to you about the Rectory that was in your region."

"If the Pope needs information from me, he can address me directly. I don't deal with underlings."

"The Pope is very busy. If you will simply tell me what happened to the Rectory and its inhabitants, I will convey that information directly to him."

"Oh, you will, will you? I don't know what happened to it. It burned. I don't know why."

"Reports are it burned with all the inhabitants locked inside. That doesn't sound like an accident."

"The region where I live is very unstable. There are lots of desperate people who are likely to do just about anything. I offered my protection, and their reply was that they were protected by the Lord. Seems he wasn't around when the place caught fire."

"You will not speak of our Lord in that manner."

Bergeron advances on him. "I will speak of anyone in any manner I choose. You asked me to come, I don't want to be here."

Frightened the bishop steps back. "I'll convey your words to the Pope."

After him, Bergeron calls out. "Tell him from here on

out I will speak only to him."

"What was that about?" Charles says.

"The church set up a rectory near my lands. I offered them my protection, but they didn't want to abide by my terms."

"Which were?"

"That I be left alone. They insisted they had to convert me and build a church on my lands. One evening, the rectory caught fire and everyone inside was killed. Now the Pope wants me to give an accounting of what happened when I don't even know myself."

"Kind of convenient for you, wasn't it?"

"It doesn't matter. They always send more. You'd think after four were hung and ten were run through with pikes, they'd realize they're operating in a volatile region."

"Quite a lot of calamities where you live. Why do you stay there?"

"I can protect myself. I can't be responsible for all these Christian warriors they keep sending."

They continue walking around the grounds until word reaches them that the Pope will speak with Bergeron and that Charlemagne's contingent has arrived, so Charles goes to pay his respects while Bergeron is lead in to see the Pope.

About fifty years after Charlemagne consolidated his kingdom, Charles finds himself in a remote region of Saxony searching for a particular home. Now a large land holder in the Frankish kingdom, he has recently been searching for acquisitions in Saxony, where, he is certain, he originated many centuries ago. Charles finds himself riding along a well-traveled roadway, looking for a standard bearing the image of a sparrow, which denotes the lands and castle of the noblewoman Katerina von Sachsen, legendary for her hospitality as well as her beauty. It is also said she likes to greet her guests with a song and this more than any other aspect fascinates Charles, himself a singer.

Arriving at the castle, Charles dismounts at the stables,

leaves his horse in the possession of a stablehand, and walks down a short path to the front door. As he does, he glances up and catches sight of the most beautiful woman he's ever set eyes on and pauses a few minutes to take in the sight. Tall and dark-haired, she's standing at an upstairs window, looking out over the lands, wearing a look of overwhelming sadness.

Charles makes no effort to attract her attention, rather he continues to the door and knocks. He's greeted by a jovial servant.

"Greetings, sir. We welcome you to our home."

"Thanks to you."

"We have supper prepared at four forty-five and it is available until seven."

"Thank you for the information. I'll be partaking."

The servant gives Charles a tour.

"I wish to pay my respects to the mistress of the house."

"Ah. My Lady typically confines herself to the upper chambers and usually only greets visitors at dinner time."

"My misfortune."

That night, Charles is seated at a long table with a few other guests. The table is laden with every delicacy he can imagine with servants bringing out more just as quickly as the guests can eat it. While they are dining, a servant announces the arrival of Katerina and Charles looks to see the beautiful woman he saw from outside descending the stairs. Now she is wearing a charming smile, but Charles can still see in her lovely green eyes the sadness he detected before.

She greets her guests: "You are welcome for as long as you need to stay and shall want for nothing while you're here. It is a custom in my family to leave you with a pleasant memory."

She nods to several musicians assembled to her left and begins an old madrigal which Charles recognizes. He is enthralled by her voice and surprised by her song selection. It is a very old song written for two singers, a man and a woman. The woman sings about finding her true love and the man answers with professions of love for her. Charles notes that she is only singing the woman's part.

When she gets to the second verse and she finishes her first part, Charles stands and in a rich baritone, replies with the man's part. Lady Katerina looks at him, startled, then a half smile crosses her face, and she continues. They finish in unison, and Lady Katerina bows slightly to Charles with a pleasant smile then exits and returns to her chambers upstairs.

After dinner, as Charles is headed to his room, a servant approaches him.

"Sir, Lady Katerina has requested your presence in her private chambers, if you wish to join her."

"I'm honored. Lead on."

Charles is led up several flights of stairs then down a long hall and into a small sitting room. Katerina rises when Charles enters and greets him in the local dialect. Charles replies with the same as he bows and introduces himself. She dismisses the servant.

"I've taken the liberty of selecting a wine for us." She pours a glass for him then returns to her seat. "I hope it's to your liking."

Charles sits then takes a sip. "It's as wonderful as your company, my Lady."

"I was rather surprised when you started singing. I wasn't aware anyone even knew that song anymore."

Charles nods. "My musical knowledge is rather extensive."

"What brings you to our lands?"

"It has been handed down in my family that we originated here many centuries ago. I've been exploring the region hoping for some clue to where that might have been."

"That's very interesting. I hope you're able to reestablish your family's connection. This is a beautiful country. I'm certain returning here would bring you much pleasure."

Charles smiles. "Not as much as an evening in your presence."

"You're too kind," Katerina says with a slight blush.

After several hours, they wrap up their conversation.

"How long will you be with us? I'd definitely appreciate an opportunity to continue our talk."

"Regretfully, I must be on my way first thing in the morning."

"My loss. I wish you safe travels."

She calls for a servant to escort him back to his quarters.

As he's leaving, he turns and calls out, "Lady Katerina?"

She looks back at him and he gazes at her for several seconds. "I just wanted a final look to carry with me."

She smiles, though Charles once again sees the sadness returning to her eyes.

The following morning, he rides away with a heavy heart, certain that he will never see her again.

Seventy-five years later, Charles finds himself once again in the region of Saxony where he first encountered Lady Katerina, and this causes him to wonder what became of her. He inquires and is surprised to hear that there is still a Katerina von Sachsen and that she's still known for her hospitality and for greeting her guests with a song. Intrigued, he arranges to spend another evening in her home.

At supper, the feast is as lavish as he remembers and at a certain point, a servant announces the arrival of Lady Katerina. As he watches her descend then move into the dining hall, Charles can do nothing more than stare in disbelief, for the woman he sees is without a doubt the same woman he met many years ago. Her face and features haven't changed at all.

She enters the dining hall and begins to greet her guests. When Lady Katerina looks toward Charles, he rises and gives a slight bow. He can tell by her expression that she recognizes him.

Charles returns to his seat and Lady Katerina goes about her usual routine.

"I've made a slight change in my song selection tonight for personal reasons." She then announces the title of the song she plans to sing; the same one she performed when Charles first met her. "It's an old song and has a part in it for a man." She surveys the crowd. "Is anyone here familiar with it?"

Charles volunteers. "I could make a feeble attempt."

When the song is finished, she thanks Charles and bids farewell to her guests and ascends back to her chambers. Once again, Charles receives an invitation to join her, and once again she dismisses her servant. This time, they go to one another and embrace.

Katerina gazes at him. "It is you, isn't it?"

"I'm as surprised as you are. How long?"

"At least three centuries. And you?"

"Five, maybe six hundred years, depending on the calendar we're using."

"I thought I was the only one."

"There are others. But I never thought I'd meet anyone like you."

They kiss.

That night, Charles doesn't return to his quarters. Within a matter of months, news filters throughout the land that Katerina is to marry a Frankish nobleman. This causes quite a stir among her subjects who have long passed about the tale of Katerina and Bartolomeo of San Lucia. It also doesn't sit well with Father Joseph, who has been convinced for years that Katerina is, in fact, the daughter of Jesus and Mary Magdalene as his predecessors relayed to him.

To address the first issue, Katerina appears with Charles before a contingent of her subjects from around the region.

"I know quite a few of you have been holding out hope that one day Bartolomeo would return and claim my hand." Tearing up, she continues. "But sadly, I have received word that Bartolomeo has fallen in battle to an infidel horde."

A mournful cry goes through the crowd.

Katerina indicates Charles. "This brave man was at Bartolomeo's side throughout the campaign and was with him when he died."

"It's true." Charles speaks solemnly. "We were set upon by a raging horde of infidels, at least two thousand—" The crowd gives a collective "Ooo." Charles continues. "Though some have claimed five thousand." This prompts an even bigger response. "Despite this, our slim forces fought bravely, never giving ground, inspired by the sight of Bartolomeo at the head of the army."

He becomes more dramatic in his gestures. "At last, we were separated as the horrid infidels launched a counter attack. I fought with my contingent until we carried the day then we hurried off to see if we could give aid to our brothers still fighting." He looks upward toward the sky with his left hand up. The crowd follows his movements, looking where he looks, and reacting whenever he gives them some gory detail. "At length, we rounded a hill and—" He breaks off his speech and covers his eyes and looks away from the crowd. "Oh, let me not relive that accursed moment."

Katerina covers her eyes and shakes her head.

"There, at the foot of the hill lay my brother in arms, Bartolomeo. Around him were the bodies of forty, maybe fifty infidels he'd bravely fought off, before one delivered a mortal blow. I went to him, cradled him and he looked up at me and made me swear an oath. He knew that he was not long for the world and his final thoughts were of his beautiful betrothed. He told me of his commitment to her and with his dying breath made me promise that I would seek her out and honor his commitment."

Several women and at least one man in the audience swoon and a few of the other men look at one another nodding.

"Now, I realize I am nowhere near the man that was Bartolomeo."

Several people in the audience yell back, "Yes you are!"

Charles acknowledges them and places his hand over his heart.

"But I swear to you on my life that I shall strive to be as good a husband as Bartolomeo would have been. He shall be my model."

At this the crowd cheers and begins clapping.

Katerina comes forward and gives Charles her hand and he drops to one knee to kiss it.

A sentimental "Aw!" goes through the crowd.

Charles and Katerina bid them good-day and return upstairs.

"That was dramatic," Katerina says.

"I believe in giving a good show."

She gives him a skeptical look. "Well, we're not out of the woods yet. How are you at convincing people you're good enough to marry the daughter of Jesus?"

He thinks it over. "Hmm, savior of all mankind, or at least that portion who believes in him. How accommodating is your priest?"

"Nothing like his predecessors. Father Stephen helped invent the myth, and his earliest successors eventually came to realize it was a hoax, but all the priests since the turn of the last century have been more dogmatic. Father Joseph truly believes he's guarding the bloodline of Christ. Now, I did try telling him you might be the beloved disciple since he supposedly lived a long time, but Joseph asked for too much proof."

"You don't skimp on your mythologizing, do you?"

She shakes her head. "You try living in close quarters with religious zealots and explain why you still look the same as you did twenty or thirty years earlier while they're starting to go gray. It's not like I had many places where I could get away."

"You will very soon."

After several meetings with Father Joseph, it becomes clear that he's in no way convinced that Charles is the right man for Katerina and will not sanction their marriage.

"I realize I don't need Father Joseph's permission or blessing, but I so want to be married in the church I built for Father Stephen. Without Joseph's sanction, that won't happen."

She and Charles spend many nights discussing it before Charles reaches the only conclusion which will settle the question once and for all.

"That's risky," Katerina says. "In fact, it's flat out dangerous."

Charles shrugs. "We have one major advantage over

these people and if we can't use that to advance our cause then what's the use of having it."

"Okay. I just hope you know what you're doing."

"You just get them out there. I'll be fine."

The following morning, a short while before sunrise, Katerina enters the church and approaches Father Joseph.

"Charles has requested an audience with you and the rest of the parish workers."

"Did he say why?"

"He says the reason will become plain once everyone is assembled."

"Very well."

Katerina leads them to the Western side of the castle, to a small hill facing the highest point of the structure, more than fifty feet. As the last of them gather, the sun is just peaking over the Eastern side of the structure.

Father Joseph looks around. "Where is Mister Renard?"

Katerina points to the top of the parapet. "There."

Father Joseph looks to see Charles standing on top of the parapet looking down at them.

"Mister Renard. Why are you up there? I thought you wanted to discuss something."

"Our discussions are ended." As he says this the sun has now climbed to just behind where he's standing. "I'm here to ask for Katerina's hand in marriage."

Father Joseph shakes his head. "I don't have the authority to grant that."

"I'm not here to ask you." He turns to face the sun. "I'm here to ask her father!"

Saying this, he spreads his arms out to his side forming the shadow of a cross before the rising sun then falls backwards off the wall. People throughout the crowd react with screams and shouts. Those who don't vocalize their shock, such as Father Joseph, simply watch in utter confusion as Charles drops through the air, crashing onto the ground. He bounces slightly then rolls to his side and becomes completely motionless. The crowd stands, staring at the sight, unable to move or even fully process what they've just witnessed.

Katerina breaks the spell as she hurries toward Charles, followed closely by Father Joseph and several of the friars.

Father Joseph kneels beside Charles' body as does one of the friars with some medical knowledge. They examine Charles a few moments before Joseph rises and addresses Katerina. "My Lady, I don't know what to say."

She stares at Charles, displaying no emotion. "Pick him up."

"Pardon?" Joseph says.

"Place him on a stretcher and take him to the church," Katerina says. "Lay him before the altar. If there's to be a sign, that's where we'll receive it."

Father Joseph eyes her with curiosity. "My Lady, are you sure?"

"Yes, and we need to hurry. There isn't much time."

Several of the monks construct a stretcher and place Charles on it. Several others rush to the church and set up a long table with some bedding on top. Once Charles' body arrives, they place him on it, closing his eyes and folding his hands across his chest. Katerina goes to the front pew and sits with her hands folded, staring intently at Charles. Father Joseph joins her and bows his head, making the sign of the cross. Slowly, more of the parish workers file in, taking their cue from Katerina, watching, sometimes praying, but mostly just staring intently at Charles' body.

A half hour passes with no activity, when suddenly, Charles's hands drop from his chest.

A monk seated in the rear stands. "Look!"

Father Joseph raises his head to see Charles' hands lying to either side of him, twitching.

People from the rear slowly start to work their way forward as Charles' entire body starts to shake then convulse before he finally presses his hands onto the table and forces himself up into a sitting position where he takes in a deep breath then relaxes slightly and looks around. Those assembled in the church stop where they are, staring at him as he slowly spins around, hanging his feet over the side of the table before hopping off. His knees start to buckle so he leans back against the table. Katerina hurries to his side putting her arm around him to help him stand.

A few moments pass before Charles looks at Father Joseph who stares in amazement at him.

Charles says, "I'll take this as consent."

Father Joseph nods. "Indeed. The Lord has made his will very plain." He leads the congregants in a cheer.

Their final obstacle overcome, Katerina and Charles begin preparing for the wedding. A few nights before it is to occur, Katerina shares some important information with Charles.

"There's something you need to know. I'm not really Katerina von Sachsen."

"What do you mean?"

She tells Charles how she came to take on the role of Katerina. "Each time the guests go on their way happy and sated and no one's ever guessed that he hasn't been in the presence of the actual Katerina."

"Au contraire. It seems to me you've been Lady Katerina a lot longer than she was."

"That is true."

"When did you discover you weren't aging?"

"Rather early. There were several girls my age in the household and by the time they were in their thirties, they'd all started to show their ages, and I hadn't. But my mother remained youthful throughout her life, and I didn't think much of it. After I became Lady Katerina, I spent less time among the servants, but when I was it was often noted that I hadn't changed much. The servants took it as some sort of sign. It wasn't until I was well into my second and third generations of servants that I realized I didn't just look younger but lived longer than the others."

"The servants all know about you?"

"They do and have for generations. Many of my current household servants are descendants of those who served the original Katerina. The secret of my longevity has been handed down. The secret of my connection to Lady Katerina has not."

"You're the only one who knows then."

"I am. Well, until you."

He considers this a moment.

"So, who were you before you were Lady Katerina?"

She smiles. "My mother always called me Renee."

Outfoxed

Since their marriage, Charles and Renee have divided their time between her manor in Saxony and his in France where they're known as the Renards. It's at the estate in France where they welcome their first child, a daughter, they name Isabella.

"Do you think she's like us?" Charles asks.

"I would imagine. Given that we both have the attribute."

"A strong argument in favor. I suppose we'll find out soon enough. Well. At least our conception of soon."

"True. Still, let's keep an eye on her, in case there are any telltale signs."

"Agreed."

They both undertake the task of instructing Isabella in reading, writing, languages, and how to defend herself. At some point in her mid-teens, she stops displaying obvious signs of aging, reassuring her parents. Half a century after Isabella's birth, at their home in Saxony, Renee gives birth to a son, Nathaniel.

One morning in 1066, a group of nobles arrives at the Renards' French estate. Charles asks that they be tended to by several of the servants while he and Renee prepare themselves to greet them. They descend to find their guests are seated around the large table in the main dining room. Charles sits at the head of the table with Renee seated against the wall behind him. He addresses the group.

"Gentlemen, to what do I owe this visit?"

The leader looks around at the others. "Mister Renard, do you believe your wife should be present?"

"Don't mind my wife. We recently married and I'm still training her on her marital responsibilities. I don't like for her to be out of my sight too long until I can be certain she's fulfilling her proper duties. She's a Saxon, though, and doesn't yet have a full grasp of our language so she won't understand what we're discussing."

Using a Saxon dialect, Renee speaks to Charles in an agitated tone. "That man is as ugly as a wart hog. He should kill himself now and spare us this hideous sight."

The nobles all look at one another and the leader says,

"What is she saying?"

"She's asking why we are meeting. Never mind her." He responds to Renee in the same dialect with an angry tone in his voice. "They don't seem to understand this dialect. Just don't use any names."

Renee throws up her hands and mumbles something more in Saxon. Then she folds her hands in her lap and says nothing more.

"Very well," the leader says. "You may be aware that William of Normandy is planning to press his case for control of Britain."

"I have heard this. I'm not sure how that concerns me."

"William needs able-bodied men to help him in this endeavor, and nobles willing to support his cause."

Charles listens in silence without betraying what is on his mind.

Another from the contingent takes up the pitch. "You come from an old and well-established family and are one of the largest landowners in the province. Your support would be most welcome by William."

"I'm sure it would. But how would it be rewarded?"

The nobles look around at one another with knowing glances. The leader continues. "Your reward will be in proportion to your generosity. England has much land and once the current ruling elite have been deposed, governance will fall to the conquerors. You'll be handsomely rewarded for your role in the endeavor."

Charles considers this. Behind him Renee speaks in Saxon in an agitated tone. "Sounds like a good deal to me."

Charles leaps out of his seat and grabs her by the arm, pulling her out of the chair.

"Please excuse me a moment."

He drags Renee out into the corridor and addresses her in Saxon, but in a low tone. "The plan does have merit. But are you willing to uproot yourself and start over again in England?"

Renee replies with an agitated tone. "We'll need to start over again somewhere sooner or later. England's as good as anywhere. Once we have land holdings there, we'll have a third place where we can bounce around to before people start to notice our attributes."

Charles nods. "Then we'll do it." He holds his hands up as if to clap them. "Let's give them the show."

Renee holds her hand up near her face. Charles counts to three and claps his hands together loudly while Renee slaps herself hard in the face and screams.

Charles follows this by shouting in French. "Never question my authority!"

He drags her back into the room and tosses her into the chair. She holds her hand to her face and looks as submissive as possible while trying not to laugh.

The nobles look around with approving smiles.

Charles remains standing. "Gentleman, would you please let William know he may count on my full support. Now, I invite you to join me in a drink so that we may toast the success of this adventure."

To prepare, Charles and Renee coordinate with Isabella and Nathaniel about how to best handle their absence. After much discussion, they determine that Nathaniel will rotate between France and Saxony to look after the family's holdings, and Isabella will be sent to a convent in Byzantium, where she can continue her studies, away from the constant gaze of nobles who may have designs on her.

On the morning of the invasion Charles, on horseback, leads a large force of men to the assembly point where they'll board boats to take them to England. Riding beside him, bearing the standard of the Renard family, is Renee, dressed as a man. William spots them and rides over to greet them.

"Charles Renard. I'm pleased that you'll be joining us in this endeavor."

"I look forward to our success, and to that end, I bring with me fifteen hundred able-bodied men ready to lay down their lives if necessary."

"You are most welcome here Mister Renard. Who is this fine lad riding with you?"

"This is Karl, my squire. A more faithful servant you won't find in this or any other country."

"Welcome to you Karl. Ready for some action today?"

Renee seems surprised and answers using a weird, highpitched voice. "I am sir."

William gives Charles an odd look. "Why does he talk like that?"

"He's, ah — been castrated."

"Castrated?"

"Yes. As a child, he was the high tenor in a boys' choir and his parents had him castrated to preserve the tone of his voice. As luck would have it the church burned down then both his parents succumbed to the plague. That's when he came into my employ."

William shakes his head. "Tough break. Well, as long as you can wield a sword, it doesn't matter what you've got downstairs."

William bids them good luck and rides off to consult his other commanders.

"Castrated?" Renee says in her normal voice.

"Well maybe if you didn't use the most ridiculous voice you can devise, I wouldn't have to come up with such outlandish stories. You have done a lower register before without any problems."

"He caught me off guard. And what's with this lay down their lives business?"

"What am I supposed to tell him, that we plan to hide behind trees until the worst of the fighting is over then ride out to take credit?"

"Good point."

When they arrive in England and the fighting gets underway, Charles and Renee employ their usual tactic of rotating their forces in and out, allowing them to engage in minor skirmishes or capture anyone who's willing to lay down their arms without engagement.

One of the other nobles senses something is amiss and approaches Charles on horseback.

"Tell me, Renard," Count Guy de Rolfe says. "Why is it your forces always seem to be at the rear of any action?"

Charles glares at him. "Given your reputation, my men are there to make sure none of yours cut and run."

De Rolfe points a sword at Charles. "Today we fight as

comrades, but once this battle is over, you'll pay for that slight to my honor."

He spins about to head back toward the fighting when an arrow pierces his chest. He sways forward and backwards once or twice then falls from his horse dead.

"So much for that," Charles says. Just then an arrow catches him and he, too, falls. Not far behind, Renee dismounts and waves over two soldiers from their troops. They drag him back to a safe place while Renee remounts and leads his horse back to where he's been taken. She dismisses the soldiers.

"Leave us. I'll tend to him."

"Tend to him?" one soldier says. "He looks pretty well dead to me."

"Looks can be deceiving. Now go back out and pretend to fight some more. Maybe try to look more aggressive to arouse less suspicion. Throw in lots of yelling."

"Yes, My Lady."

By the time Charles recovers, word has circulated that he has fallen in battle. Twenty minutes later, William is surprised when he encounters Charles rallying his men for a second attack.

"Renard? I heard you were killed."

Charles gives a spirited guffaw. "Well, I'm all better now. Let's hit them again and we may win this day."

"I like your spirit."

"Oh, by the way, Count de Rolfe did fall in battle. I was at his side, and he implored me to lead his troops and made me swear an oath that they would share in whatever rewards attended his service. I'm certain others heard this."

"That's quite all right. De Rolfe was a fine warrior, and his wishes will be fulfilled."

Charles and Renee at first have trouble convincing de Rolf's soldiers to abide by their orders to stay out of the main fighting. Charles states the case more forcefully.

"I assume many of you have families."

Most of the men respond with a yes.

"Wouldn't you like to see them again, maybe watch your children grow up?"

This convinces the holdouts.

"I have it on reliable authority that Count de Rolf put in a good word for you, which may lead to favorable consequences."

Once the battle is finished and the prizes are being awarded, the Foxes receive a thousand acres in and around Kent. De Rolfe's soldiers are each rewarded with an acre and a half of land, divided from among the holdings he was promised. They all sing the praises of their fallen leader who they herald as "Guy the Benevolent".

"Not bad for a day's fighting," Renee tells Charles.

Isabella hurries through the corridors of the convent where she has spent a significant portion of her life, which is now more than two hundred years. She received an urgent message from the Mother Superior as she was at her morning studies, stating she was needed. The Sisters are mostly aware of Isabella's attributes and have protected the secret for as long as she has been here.

She enters the Mother Superior's chamber and kneels. "You needed to see me, Mother?"

"Please rise, Belle. There's a critical matter I must discuss with you."

Isabella rises and moves toward the Mother Superior. "What is it, Mother?"

The Mother Superior gazes out the window. "Come over here."

Isabella goes to the window, looks out, and gasps. Along the edge of the hill away from the convent is a long row of pikes, each containing the nude body of a woman.

Tears come to her eyes, and she turns away from the horrid sight. "Who would do such an inhuman thing."

"Someone who those in the region believe may not be human."

The Mother Superior walks to a bench but stands beside it without sitting.

"I don't understand."

The Mother Superior does not immediately respond but remains in silent thought.

"Mother, what's this about? What do you mean by someone who isn't human?"

"Are you able to summon your father, Belle?"

Isabella shakes her head. "No, Mother, my parents went to England with William in the last century. I've not heard from them for many years.

"What about your brother, Nathaniel?"

"I could write to him, but it could take months before he'll arrive. He's been minding our family's holdings in Saxony. If his presence is required, I need to summon him now."

"We may not have the time. When he gets here, all he may find are ashes."

"Is it the marauders? Are they the ones who've done this?"

"They are but a small part of the problem. It is said they serve a dark Lord, known only as Bergeron. He inhabits a castle miles away and dispatches his men to harass the order."

"That name is familiar. My father has mentioned him, but never warned me to avoid him. He obviously hasn't remained in contact, though. I don't know why."

"People in the region say he's a fierce warrior who has conquered death. He's been killed many times, yet rises from the dead, more powerful than before."

Isabella looks at the floor. "Of course. If he's like me. I assure you, he's very much human."

The Mother Superior turns toward the window. "A week ago, we sent an envoy to ask for his mercy. That's them on the hill. Only one was allowed to live, mainly to convey a warning to the rest of us. With the horrors she endured, her sisters are the lucky ones." She pulls the drapes shut then moves away from the window. "I fear word may have left the convent that you're here. The sisters are trustworthy, but some have relatives in the surrounding area who aren't so discreet. Whether he knows you're here or not, we do not have much time. His attacks have grown more brazen and now that he's murdered our envoys, he has no reason to conceal that he's behind the attacks."

"Isn't there anything we can do?"

"There's an order some distance away that's better fortified and under the protection of a Duke who favors them. If we could make it to them, we can survive, but if we attempt to travel alone—"

"I'll summon Nathaniel. Then I'll go see Bergeron since it seems to be me he wants. I may not be able to stop him, but perhaps I can buy enough time for Nathaniel to get here."

"If you're certain." Isabella lowers her head, then nods. "Bless you, Belle. It may be the only hope we have."

Roland Fox had every opportunity to make something of his life. The younger of Charles and Renee's two sons, he learned from a very early age that he would most likely have a long time to decide what he wanted to do with himself. By the time he reached age sixty he realized his parents' pronouncements had proven true as he still looked like he was in his late teens. Born at his parent's manor in England a few years before his father and other nobles forced King John to sign the Magna Charta, Roland spent the first two hundred and fifty years of his life in his parents' household. His older siblings, Isabella and Nathaniel had established themselves as landowners on the continent, and Roland's twin sister Katherine was pursuing an acting career.

Though his parents never applied any pressure on him to move out or get on with his life, he felt they would like to see him working toward some goal, so Roland decided to go the scholarly route. He headed off to Oxford where he studied the classics, learned Greek and Latin, and was generally bored to tears. While he had planned to work on a degree in Philosophy, he ended up dropping out and hanging around London then touring the continent a time or two, trying to find something to spur his interest.

One afternoon, lounging around his flat, he hits upon an idea, and puts together a master con job. He rounds up investors for a proposed settlement in the "new world" and gives such a good performance, that he has deep pockets lined up around the block to buy in.

"How long do you anticipate it will be until we see profits?"

"Oh, friends, not for a year or more." Roland rises and illustrates his speech with dramatic gestures. "The travel alone can take many months, and in some of these ports, it's difficult to know who's waiting or how they will receive the newcomers. I anticipate many months of negotiations, but once we settle in and begin to reap the benefits of these distant partnerships, the rewards will begin rolling in at a staggering rate."

Many are skeptical, but an equal number are eager to take Roland up on his challenge and before long, he's flush with cash and assurances of more once he produces results. At last, he bids farewell to his benefactors and sets out for the colony with promises that he will return with an update and the first profits. Instead, he sails to Amsterdam, where he lives off his ill-gotten gain for many years, until he is sure most of his financiers have died.

Certain that he's hit on the perfect scam, Roland heads to Paris, where he has equal success in conning investors, and this time he hides out in Milan. He'd last hit England in the late 1700s, so by the mid-19th century, Roland is sure the coast is clear. He returns and once again sets out to gather investors, and is equally successful, though his original spiel of populating the "new world" has to undergo some modifications, given the uprising in the American colonies at the end of the last century.

"Our plan is to colonize Fiji," he tells one group. "There's only a small group of natives to deal with, and we're pretty sure we can overtake them without much trouble."

One prospective investor asks, "What will you do with them?"

Roland raises his finger and chuckles. "Oh, rest assured, my friend, we have a plan." He taps his nose, which causes several of the investors to nod knowingly.

For another group of investors, he rolls out a different spiel: "For this excursion, we'll be leasing diamond mines in Africa."

"When you say 'leasing' do you mean you'll pay them or they'll pay you?"

"Why they'll pay us."

"Who exactly will you be charging?"

"The Dutch, of course."

"Don't they already own the mines?"

"That's the genius of the plan. We get them coming and going."

In yet another pitch, Roland tries a new approach.

"You, my friends, have the exclusive priviledge to invest in an exciting venture we're calling Even Newer South Wales!"

One afternoon in 1861, Roland is in his flat when he hears a knock at the door. He answers to find one of his creditors accompanied by a constable.

"That's him." The creditor wags his finger at Roland. "That's the man."

"What's this about?"

"Mr. Fox, this gentleman says you owe him a considerable sum of money."

"I wouldn't call it 'considerable'. Besides, I intend to make good on it very soon."

"He owes me £500."

The constable nods. "I'd call that a considerable sum, sir."

"And he's been saying he'd pay me for more than a year. Yesterday an associate saw him at a shipping company making arrangements for what appeared to be a long trip."

"Is this true, sir?"

Roland shrugs. "My business takes me all over the world."

"What business is that, exactly?"

"I secure financing for various overseas ventures. I guess you could say I'm a speculator."

"Speculating on how to rob people blind is more like it. I know this neighborhood and it costs a pretty penny for a flat here."

The constable considers it all for a moment. "Would you please accompany us down to the precinct to sort this out, Mr. Fox."

"Today is awfully busy. Could I pop by tomorrow some-time?"

"I'm afraid that wasn't a request, Mr. Fox." The con-stable takes Roland by the arm. "Please come with me."

Once in custody, the authorities publicize Roland's name and description and within forty-eight hours, four hundred and twenty-nine people come forward claiming to have lost money in one of his get-rich-quick schemes. One ancient man, stooped and leaning heavily on a walk-ing stick, gives Roland a stern examination before shak-ing his cane at him.

"Aye! That's the scoundrel. I'll ne'er forget his face. He swindled me out of me family's fortunes when I was but a young lad in 1784!"

"Sir, that's impossible. This man is hardly twenty-five years old."

"It's him, I tell you. The same scurvy dog what cheated me out of everything."

"Then perhaps we're dealing with a family of swin-dlers."

Despite the mountain of evidence against him, Ro-land remains stony and unrepentant, refusing even to acknowledge his guilt or innocence. At last, his sentence is handed down. He's to be transported to Australia for hard labor and in the meantime, he'll be held in debtors' prison.

On his first day there, Roland is seated in the main yard when he looks up to see his twin sister Katie enter-ing. She's dressed in an old and worn homespun dress with an apron over top of it. Her hair is mussed, and she appears to have been crying. While Roland looks more like his mother, with dark hair and greenish eyes, Katie more closely resembles their father, but with ash brown hair and gray eyes. Seeing Roland, she thrusts her folded hands in front of her face and begins to cry again.

"Oh, dear brrrruther!" Katie speaks with an inexplica-bly bad accent that sounds vaguely Irish. "I din't wanna believe 'em, but 'tis true!"

She throws her hands out beside her then wraps them

around Roland and begins to wail and sob.

"Good god, Katie. What's with all the dramatics. And why are you wearing this getup."

She continues to embrace him but speaks in her normal voice with a note of sarcasm. "It seemed the proper attire for visiting one's brother in debtor's prison."

"Point taken. By the way, your Irish still needs a lot of work."

"That was Scottish."

"Then it really needs some work."

She releases him and they sit on a nearby bench.

"Have you spoken to Mom and Dad?"

"Yes. They're hoping you have a lovely time in Australia."

"Oh, come on, they're not going to actually let this happen are they?"

"Mom was livid. Dad couldn't even calm her down. You're lucky he convinced her to let me come to see you. They'll tolerate a lot of things, but scamming most of England for over three hundred years is beyond the pale, even for you."

"It's not like I hurt anyone."

"Roland, you've been taking people's money then leaving the country until all your creditors die then you come back and do it all over. I don't know if there are actual rules for long-timers, but if there are, that one's sure to be in the top ten of the prohibited column."

He shrugs and shakes his head.

"Did you at least talk to my friend, Johnny Baynes? He's normally strapped for cash but can usually scrounge some up when needed."

"Oh yes, Johnny Baynes. He'll most likely be accompanying you on your little excursion."

Roland is genuinely surprised. "What? What happened?"

"He got caught breaking into some shop. That and numerous nuisance complaints, not to mention something about an explosion have earned him a ticket down under."

"Well, at least I'll have someone to commiserate with.

Might not be so bad after all."

"You and Johnny Baynes romping around Australia. The aborigine won't know what hit them."

A greasy looking man in a worn topcoat walks nearby and addresses Katie. "Got time for a quick one, love?"

Katie leaps to her feet, points at him, and yells with a thick Cockney accent. "You watch yourself now. I'm a respectable lady."

"Shove off, Wally. This is my sister."

"Oh!" The man bows and moves away.

"Your cockney's getting better."

Katie sits beside him again. "Thanks. I've been working on it."

Roland shakes his head. "You're not still hanging around Aldgate are you?"

"Just during the day, but one of these days, I intend to immerse myself in the area. Learn how the other half really lives."

"Do you honestly think that helps with your acting?"

She shrugs. "I don't know. It's fun, though. Like stepping outside my skin for a while."

"Anymore run-ins with that McIntyre woman and you may step out of your skin permanently."

Katherine laughs. "I can handle Sally McIntyre. She just caught me off guard last time."

"Well, just watch out. Situations have a way of getting out of hand."

"You're one to talk, Mister Never Consider the Consequences of His Actions. I shudder to think how many little Rolands and Rolandas are running around out there."

He scowls and looks away from her. "You know, maybe you have the right idea after all. I wish I could step outside my skin for a while."

"Seems you've been doing quite a lot of that lately. Maybe a trip down under will do you some good."

"Like a dose of arsenic,"

"Oh, come on. It'll all be over before you know it. Then you can get on with your life and this will all just fade into the background."

"The sooner the better."

Francis Tremaine enters the convalescent ward of a makeshift hospital in Elizabethan London and moves through the rows of patients whose bodies show the unmistakable signs of plague, blackening along their extremities and swollen patches of skin around their necks, arms, and legs. He pauses a moment near the bed of a patient named Graeme he'd seen a day or so earlier, who seems to be recovering. Francis surveys the ward, pleased with the condition of the room in which the patients are housed. Though crowded, it's neat and tidy, the floors well-scrubbed, and while Francis detects the telltale scent of death, it does not hang in the air as it does in other facilities elsewhere in the city. The reason for this, he well knows, is the presence of the woman known as "Sister Eleanor" to those fortunate enough to find themselves under her care.

Francis knows her as Eleanor Goolsby.

He quickly scans the room then heads toward the back where Eleanor keeps her living quarters. In the weeks since discovering this facility, Francis has become increasingly interested in Eleanor, her dedication to easing the suffering of her charges, her tireless devotion to making a difference in the lives of those who are ill, but most of all, what intrigues him is how she manages to stay healthy, despite living among the sickest of individuals.

He walks to the end of the ward and taps at the door. A moment passes before it opens a crack and Eleanor peers out.

"Oh, Dr. Tremaine." She opens the door to admit him. "I wasn't expecting you again so soon."

"I had business in London and thought I'd look in on you. I see Graeme is doing better."

"Yes sir. The poor man has had a tough go of it, but he does seem to have turned the corner."

Francis examines Eleanor. She is taller than average and thin but does not appear undernourished. Her chestnut brown hair is pulled back away from her face and secured under a white scarf and her clothing is plain and unadorned. As she speaks, she nervously fiddles with her hands.

"I must commend you, Eleanor. There aren't many who'd devote so much of their time to helping the sick the way you have."

"The same could be said of you, sir. Many of the doctors I've encountered seem more concerned with counting the bodies than figuring out how to help those in need."

"I only wish there was more I could do. The conventional remedies have proven totally ineffective. A colleague of mine raised an interesting point a few days ago. He stated that he has seen fewer manifestations of the plague in areas where the rodent population is less. He believes there may be a connection but has yet to conjecture on what."

"Yes sir. I try to keep those nasty critters out of my rooms. They just frighten me, sir. Do you know that a small child a few streets over was attacked in her sleep by a horde of rats one evening? They're disgusting."

Francis walks to the rear of Eleanor's quarters and runs his eyes over her meager belongings, a rosary, some coins, and a tiny crucifix.

"How are you faring, Eleanor? No fever, no outward signs of the illness?"

"Oh, no sir. I'm as healthy as an ox."

"I see that." He turns back to face her. "It doesn't affect you, does it?"

"Affect me, sir? Of course, it affects me. To look at all that suffering and not feel something, one would have to be very heartless indeed."

"That's not what I meant. You don't get sick, do you?"

Eleanor turns away from him and lowers her head. "Well, sir, the good Lord has certainly blessed me."

"No, I think it's more than that. I'm curious about something, Eleanor. Do you know when you were born?"

She gives him a frightened look. "Why would you want to know about my birth, sir?"

"Just a question that came to me after my last visit."

"I can't rightly say, sir. My parents weren't very good at keeping those sorts of records."

"Then perhaps you can tell me, who was on the throne when you were born?"

Eleanor turns away from Francis and moves away from him with a pained expression on her face.

"Why are you asking me these questions, doctor? Why is my birth so important to you?"

"I'll explain my reasons once you tell me who was on the throne when you were born. Surely your mother knew that."

Eleanor refuses to face him and continues wringing her hands. "Of course, she knew, sir. She told me many times when I was a small child."

"Who was it?"

She turns toward him, her eyes wet with tears.

"It was Henry, sir, Henry Tudor — the seventh, not the eighth."

"Really." Francis scans her with much interest.

"Yes sir. That's what my mother told me. She said I was born within a fortnight of Prince Henry's birth."

He does the math in his head. "Why that would make you eighty-six years old, Eleanor."

"Is that right, sir? Then I suppose I am."

Francis considers this.

"It may interest you to know, that I was born under Henry as well."

Eleanor eyes him with curiosity. "Sir? You were born under Henry?"

"I was, Eleanor. Henry of Monmouth."

She looks at him with a shocked expression.

"Henry the Fifth? But sir that would make you more than a hundred."

"A hundred and sixty, to be exact, Eleanor. I don't get sick either — neither does my sister."

"Your sister, Bethany."

"She's just a few years younger than I am."

He walks over and takes her hands. Eleanor is crying and Francis places his hand on her cheek and smiles.

"You see, Eleanor, you're not alone."

"Oh sir, I don't know what's brought you to me, but this is a great blessing. I never imagined I'd meet another like me."

"No more of this sir business. My friends call me Francis."

Francis invites Eleanor back to the home he shares with his sister in London and a few days afterward Eleanor accepts their offer to move into their spare bedroom provided she can continue to run her clinic.

Bergeron is dining alone when a servant enters and bows to him. "Lord Bergeron, forgive this intrusion, but there's a messenger here to see you."

"A messenger from whom?"

"I do not know my Lord. She will only speak to you."

"She?"

"Yes, my Lord. She's dressed as a man, but her voice and form are female."

"Then she's from the convent."

"I cannot say, my Lord. Her words are for you alone."

Bergeron considers this, then rises. "Very well. I could use some entertainment with dinner. Assemble a crew who are suitably amorous."

"Yes, my Lord."

He follows the servant back to the main hall of the castle. There, a solitary figure waits near the door, guarded by two of Bergeron's men. The person is dressed as the servant described, in dark, loose clothing, with a hood over her head and a kerchief pulled up to conceal part of the face.

"Let me guess, you're here to plead for the safety of the convent."

"I'm here to offer a compromise." She makes no attempt to disguise her voice.

"Last time, they sent twenty-four. Nearly exhausted all our available pikes. At least we won't waste so many resources disposing of you."

"Will you not, at least, hear me out?"

"What could you possibly have to offer of any value to me? Get her out of here. What you do with her afterward is your business."

The men seize and drag her toward the door, but just as they come within a few feet of it, her body suddenly goes completely limp, straining their arms.

"Get up!" Both men roughly jerk her up, raising her off the ground.

She uses the momentum to put her foot against the door, then walks up the wall and pushes hard backward, flipping over and breaking the grip the men have on her. She lands, rolls once, springs to her feet, then sprints across the floor and grabs a staff leaning against the wall. The men are caught off guard, but recover and draw their swords, and aggressively approach her. Bergeron watches intently.

She stands her ground, holding the staff in a defensive position until the men are nearly upon her, then she swings the staff toward the legs of one of the men, knocking him off balance. The second man lunges at her, but she sidesteps, and jams the staff into his side, which brings him to his knees. She spins around and brings the staff down on his arm, causing him to drop his sword. She follows up by smashing him in the head, which renders him unconscious, then she dives for the sword, retrieving it, then getting to her feet to face the first man, who's recovered. She holds onto the hilt firmly as the man attacks, unable to disarm her.

By now, more of Bergeron's men have assembled, and they draw their swords, but Bergeron signals to them not to intervene. The man attacking her makes another pass, this time swinging wildly, trying to disarm her. She raises her sword to block his move, and they stand, him pressing down against her blade, while she struggles to hold him off. Then she kicks him hard in the groin, causing him to double over in pain, and she spins around and slices his neck with her blade. He falls to the floor dead.

Bergeron nods and more of his men rush her, but she suddenly drops to her knees, and thrusts her sword upward, impaling one man, then taking his sword in her other hand. Two more men advance toward her. She drops the swords, and cartwheels over to where the staff lies and picks it up, using it to fend off the two attackers.

"Enough!" Bergeron finally says. The woman maintains her defensive posture as the two men stand down.

Bergeron walks up behind them. "Take these bodies away."

The men follow his orders. Bergeron stares at the woman with a half-smile on his face.

"Very impressive. I doubt the Sisters taught you that."

"I haven't always lived in a convent."

"You have my attention. What else can you do?"

In reply, she lets go of the staff, then takes down her hood and mask and appears to be extremely young. She pulls up her sleeve and presents her forearm to him. "I understand you have a test."

"That's not the test."

"I know, but I'd rather not have my throat cut if it's all the same to you."

Bergeron takes out a knife, then grabs her arm and slices it just below the elbow. She grimaces as blood pours from the wound but does not cry out. In a few moments, the cut heals itself. Bergeron puts away the knife.

"There have been rumors floating around the region that they've been protecting someone who couldn't die. How long?"

"A century or more at least."

"What do you want? I must assume you're here to make some sort of deal."

"I want you to leave the Sisters alone. If it's me you want, neither you, nor your men can bother them any longer. You don't have to extend your protection, just cease your harassment."

"And what do I get in return?"

"A companion who'll live for as long as you will. Who'll be by your side long after these others have turned to dust."

He eyes her with suspicion. "How do I know this isn't a trick?"

"You don't, but I'll earn your trust, I'm confident of that."

Bergeron motions toward the rear door.

"I was just dining. Join me, and we'll discuss this further. What are you called?"

"The Sisters call me Belle."

"What do you know about your parentage?"

"Very little. I recall a rather animated man and woman who used to dote on me and taught me how to defend myself when I was a youngster."

"What became of them?"

"There was trouble in the village near where we lived, and they sent me away to the convent for protection. I later learned that the villagers had discovered the secret of their lifespans and believed them to be demons or vampires and murdered them."

"Not the worst thing that can happen to one of us."

"Their bodies were burned."

"That would do it. You say you were sent away. From where?"

"Saxony. My parents had the foresight to send me far away. Perhaps one day, I'll have a partner who can help me regain the lands they lost."

"Perhaps."

They enter the dining hall, and Bergeron addresses the servant standing by. "Bring another plate for our guest."

He motions to the table. Belle sits at the opposite end away from him. The servant returns and sets a plate in front of her laden with meat and local vegetables.

"Quite a feast." She raises her fork and knife. "They don't eat like this at the convent."

"I imagine not." He consumes a few morsels without removing his eyes from her. "You do realize what I'll expect from you if you remain here."

"I do. It may take some time, but I can adapt to that role."

"If you truly value your charges at the convent, you'll do so quickly."

"Understood."

"Very well. We shall try this and see how it works."

The Foxes' household servants are gathered around the courtyard at the estate in Kent, watching as Charles and Renee practice with their swords. When they married, Charles was pleased to find that Renee was familiar with the use of a sword, though her technique was rough having only practiced with reluctant servants who may not have given their best efforts due to who their opponent was. Charles himself was largely self-taught until he could afford to bring in more polished trainers to learn better technique. Since their marriage, he and Renee meet two or three times a week to fence and work out any kinks. Renee's proficiency is equal to Charles's and frequently the servants take bets on who'll prevail.

Usually, Katherine and Roland practice with them, but they've taken residence at the family's lodgings in London for several weeks at their parents' insistence. These precautions, as well as this week's sessions have a special urgency to them, because Renee and Charles have visitors coming, and one of those visitors, Danforth Mortimer, has a reputation for taking advantage of the hospitality of those who host him.

Charles describes him as they parry back and forth: "He's a low-grade nobleman somehow related to the Earl of March, though exactly how is anybody's guess. His land holdings in the region rival ours."

"I thought you were the one who's going to fight him."

"I will be, but we also need to be sure your skills are honed, in case something unexpected happens. Remember, he's very crafty and I hear he likes to cheat."

He lunges, but Renee sidesteps and knocks the blade away. He salutes. "Very good. You've come a long way since the days of fighting servants in the back hallways."

"I hope so. I've had a few hundred years to improve."

From the tower a horn sounds to announce the approach of riders in the distance. They salute one another, put away the weapons, then Charles and Renee hurry inside to freshen up. They hop on a pair of horses and ride out to greet their guests. Watching as the noblemen move within sight range, Renee puts her hand over her face. "Which one is Mortimer?"

Charles pretends to wipe his cheek with the back of his hand. "Black beard with silver slivers."

"He looks awfully lecherous. You've heard what he did to Lady Ashton."

"That is why I'll be keeping a close watch on him. Just remember, be friendly but not obviously friendly."

"Got it."

The nobles ride up and Charles removes his hat. "Gentlemen, you are welcome here. And may I assure you that while you remain under our roof, you will want for nothing."

As he's speaking, Renee allows her gaze to move to Mortimer and as she imagined, he's looking intently at her.

From that moment, every time Renee is in close contact with Mortimer, she shoots him suggestive glances or gives him a seductive smile. It takes a day or so, but finally Renee looks around to see Mortimer is shadowing her. She gives a slight whistle which is a signal to Charles. Mortimer corners Renee in an alcove and moves in.

"My Lady, you have bewitched me. I am no longer in control of myself."

"Mr. Mortimer, please. I am a respectable woman."

"Respect isn't what's on my mind right now."

He puts his arms around her.

"I should say not!" Charles appears behind them. Mortimer jumps then turns to face Charles as Renee hurries to where he's standing. He points at her and speaks to a couple of servants. "See to my wife."

By now several of the other nobles have arrived. Charles pulls his gloves from his belt.

"Sir, you would insult me in my own house?" He angrily throws his gloves at Mortimer's feet then takes one step forward. "If you are truly a man of honor and not the sniveling dog you have just demonstrated yourself to be, you'll pick those up.

He points at the gloves and stares directly into Mortimer's eyes.

Mortimer glares at him then reaches down and picks up the gloves. Charles nods.

"Very good. We'll settle this in one hour." He looks around at those assembled. "Because I am a man of honor, I will allow you your choice of weapon."

Mortimer smirks. "A fatal mistake on your part."

"We shall see."

Charles hurries off in the direction Renee was taken. She's waiting around the corner.

"Sniveling dog?"

"His pride is easily bruised. I knew once I called him that, he'd have no choice but to accept."

"I'm told he's one of the finest swordsmen in the land. Are you sure this is such a good idea?"

"I heal quicker. Plus I have a thousand years of experience on him."

At the appointed hour, Charles and Mortimer square off across from one another. Mortimer chooses rapiers and both take one and test them.

Charles says to him, "Next time I see Roger at court, I'll suggest he disown you."

"I doubt you'll see him again at court, because you won't be there."

Charles and Mortimer salute one another then begin fighting. From the start, Charles is the aggressor, keeping Mortimer mostly off-balance and on the defensive. At one point, Mortimer lunges but Charles sidesteps then spins around and gets the drop on him. Mortimer manages to extricate himself but it's not long before he finds himself in trouble again. During a flurry of activity, Charles disarms Mortimer then places his blade against Mortimer's throat.

"It would appear, sir, I have bested you."

"It would appear. But can you handle two more?"

Two of Mortimer's men draw their swords behind Charles.

"I knew it! I knew you'd cheat. Didn't I say he'd cheat, Renee?"

Suddenly, one of Mortimer's men cries out and falls dead to the ground. Behind him, Renee stands with a sword and wearing pantaloons. "I owe you a pound sterling."

"What is the meaning of this? You expect me to believe your wife can best my remaining man?"

"You should believe she can best you as well. But today you're mine." He retrieves Mortimer's rapier and tosses it to him. "Have at you!"

Renee faces off with Mortimer's remaining man and she's as aggressive as Charles is with Mortimer. Finally, she lunges to deliver a fatal thrust then she and Charles back Mortimer up against a wall.

"I ask only that you finish me off quickly."

Charles lowers his sword. "I plan to show you more restraint than you did Lady Ashton. You'll at least leave here alive."

He turns to Renee. "Say the word, darling, and I'll give you his family jewels to wear as a necklace."

Renee makes a sour face. "That is disgusting. Just take his land."

"Ah yes. Sign your land over to me and never visit this region of England again and we'll call this matter settled."

Mortimer glares at him. "Very well."

Another noble prepares the papers which Charles and Mortimer sign with the others as witnesses.

"Now, Mortimer, you have one day to vacate our house, our lands, and this region. If you're still here the following sunrise I'll finish the job we started here."

Several weeks later, the Foxes host the children of Lady Ashton and sign over rights to the land Mortimer stole from them. Mortimer never has a chance to avenge the insult, as he gets swept away in an epidemic of the plague that goes through later that year.

Bethany Tremaine goes downstairs at her London residence and enters the kitchen. There, she finds Eleanor Goolsby seated at the table with a bowl of what appears to be porridge in front of her. Eleanor is leaning on one arm with her eyes focused away from the table, deep in thought.

"Good morning, Eleanor."

Eleanor jumps at the sound of Bethany's voice, then looks at her and titters as she twists her head sideways.

"Good morning, Miss— I'm sorry. Bethany. I'm afraid I was a bit lost in my thoughts."

She focuses on her breakfast and samples a spoonful.

"You're a very thoughtful person. Quite understandable."

Bethany fills a kettle with water and places it on the stove. Then she spoons several teaspoons of black tea into a pot and sets it near the stove. She joins Eleanor at the table.

"I'm sorry you couldn't join Francis and me at the theater last evening. The show was spectacular."

"Yes, ma'am— I mean— Bethany. I was worried about one of my charges at the hospital, so I went by to check on him and lost track of time."

"I admire your dedication, Eleanor." She raises her finger. "But you should always be sure to set aside time for yourself as well. The world can usually take care of itself for one evening."

"I know. I just don't feel comfortable enjoying myself when there's so many in need. I worry whenever I'm away from the hospital for long stretches."

"You're new to all this. No need to worry. I'm sure that once you've settled into a new routine, you'll start to relax and see that things will be all right."

"I certainly hope so."

"I trust that the assistant Francis hired is pulling his weight."

"Oh, indeed. He has been a great blessing. It does ease my worries knowing he's there in my absence."

The kettle starts to whistle and Bethany goes to the stove and removes it from the heat, then fills the teapot with it and puts on the lid.

"How long have you been taking care of people, Eleanor? I asked Francis and he wasn't sure."

"I can hardly imagine a time when I wasn't, if you must know. My mother realized when I was very young that I wasn't like my other siblings. They all died young."

"I'm sorry to hear that. Then you were the only one with your abilities."

"That's right. My mother outlived several husbands. I was the daughter of her second and she had two others after that one. No children by the first. Several after me."

"You say your mother figured out you weren't like the

others."

"Yes. Several rather nasty plagues occurred in our area, and I never came down with them, though I was exposed to many who succumbed to them."

"That would be a giveaway, but what set you apart? There are others with regular lifespans who can withstand illnesses."

"My mother told me that when I was a very small child, I was run over by a cart. I was playing in the road with some other children and a driver came around the corner going too quickly and didn't see us. Me and two other children were trampled by the horses, and I was run over by one of the wheels."

"That's awful."

"The other children died instantly, and my mother was certain I'd soon join them. She took me into the house and laid me in my bed and held vigil over me expecting me to pass. Instead, she said I recovered before her eyes. My cuts and bruises just vanished and in less than an hour, there was no sign anything had happened to me."

"Amazing. How did she react?"

"Frankly, she told me she was frightened."

"Frightened?" Bethany considers it a moment. "Yes. Actually, I can see that. Especially since you were in such bad shape before. It would certainly be difficult to explain."

"Yes. She told me she fretted over it for quite a while and finally, she bundled me up and took me to a relative's home some distance away. She told those in our neighborhood that I had died, and was buried in our family's plot in another county."

"Probably not a terrible idea."

"After a time, she married her third husband and they relocated to another part of London, so she brought me there to live."

"Incredible. I had no idea you'd gone through so much at such a young age."

"My mother was never quite the same after that. I mean I only have vague recollections of our time together since I was so young, but I do recall her being very affectionate, singing to me, hugging me. No more of that. It was like she was afraid to even touch me."

"How did that lead to your caregiving?"

"As I say, my brothers and sisters all succumbed at an early age to the various illnesses that came along. Because I wasn't affected, it became my job to take care of them."

"You're mother did that to you?"

"She told me it must be my purpose. Otherwise why had I been given this gift."

"That's an awful lot of responsibility for a young girl."

"It was. But I found it difficult to argue with her. No matter how sick someone else was, I never came down with it. Plague, pox, typhus. It made no difference. I could withstand it. I eventually cared for my entire family."

"Even your mother?"

"Her, too. On her deathbed, she told me I wasn't like everyone else and must keep that very quiet or else people might believe I'm a demon or cursed. It was some years after she died that I realized I didn't seem to be getting older as well. That just settled for me that it must be supernatural as she suggested. However I came by it, I decided to use it and the resources left me to make a difference for those who weren't as fortunate."

Bethany lays her hand on Eleanor's. "It sounds to me like you've earned a respite. Let Francis and me show you how to enjoy yourself."

"I'd be obliged, Bethany. All I can ever remember is serving others. I'm not sure I know how to go about putting myself ahead of that."

"Slowly. A little at a time. You'll start to sort it out and we're here to help you every step of the way."

One morning Renee and Charles are seated at the table in their London home. Charles is drinking coffee, while Renee is reading the paper. An item on the front page immediately catches her eye.

"Charles. It says here that someone's assassinated that lovely Mr. Lincoln." She lowers the paper and looks at him with a sad expression.

Charles shakes his head. "Do they know who did it?"

Renee reads a bit more and gasps. "They say Wilkes did it."

"Wilkes Booth?"

"Yes. It says Lincoln was watching Our American Cousin—"

"You'd have thought he'd have a better sendoff than that."

"—at Ford's Theater, when Wilkes shot him from behind then jumped onto the stage and ran away."

"Figures. Wilkes was always the one to overdramatize things. Poor Edwin — you know he'll catch hell for this."

"You don't think Edwin is involved, do you?"

"Of course not. But you know how people are. Damn shame. It's not his fault his brother's an idiot."

Renee looks back to the account. "He's now a dead idiot. It says he was killed while hiding on someone's farm."

Charles thinks about something for a moment then chuckles. "I'll bet you a sovereign I can tell you how it went inside the theater — Wilkes creeping up the stairs reciting Cassius' lines from Caesar 'How many ages hence...'" He shakes his head.

Renee nods. "He probably thought he'd be heralded as some sort of hero. It says here that people on both sides of the American conflict helped in the hunt for him."

"Wilkes should have reminded himself of Antony's lines. 'The evil that men do lives after them. The good is oft interred with their bones.'"

"We should invite Edwin and his daughter over for a visit. Get them away from the furor — maybe get his mind off everything."

"I'll send him a letter."

Just then, their daughter Katherine comes in, somewhat out of breath, her hair messy and clothing a bit ruffled.

"Katie, what's happened to you?" Renee says.

Katie looks at them with uncertainty. "Nothing. I'm going to my room." She turns to go to her room, but then turns back. "Oh, if a woman named Sally comes looking for me, say you don't know me, okay?"

"Katherine what have you gotten yourself into now?" Charles says.

She turns to look at them again then sighs loudly and sits at the table.

"As you know, I've been hanging around the East End to pick up the local vernacular."

Charles throws up his hands and Renee covers her face, saying, "Not again."

"I'm learning a lot," Katie protests. "I've gotten so I fit right in, which is sort of the problem."

"Let's hear it," Renee says.

"There's this woman, Sally McIntyre. I'd had a run in with her a few weeks ago and she told me to stay away from her 'territory' as she put it. So earlier, I was out wandering around one of the neighborhoods, and I saw her again. She recognized me and wasn't very happy to see me, so she chased me several blocks. I managed to elude her, but I'm worried she or one of her cohorts might have seen me come this way."

"What have we told you?" Renee says.

"I know. I don't go there looking for trouble."

"You don't need to look for trouble there," Charles says. "It finds you. Have you figured out what you're going to do about this Sally person?"

"It seems there's only one thing I can do that will settle this. I do wish Roland was still here. I could always count on him to watch my back."

"Well, I'm afraid you're on your own this time," Renee says.

Katie gets up and goes toward her room. "I guess I'd better get ready."

Henry Tudor has been biding his time, waiting for the opportunity to return to England to press his claim to the throne. The leader of the House of Lancaster, it is his intention to put an end to the conflicts once and for all and establish his own dynasty which he hopes will rule England forever, but which will likely burn itself out in a little over a century leading to some distant Scottish cousin taking the throne. But Henry isn't here to think about such things, he's here to defeat Richard on the field of battle and institute his rule over England.

As his forces advance toward Bosworth Field, they encounter a large troop of men assembled in a nonconfrontational manner. At the head of the forces is an individual Henry knows, Charles Fox. He and his standard bearer approach Henry on horseback.

"Fox, what the devil are you doing here?"

"I thought you might be able to use an additional fifteen hundred able-bodied men. We're here to help you press your claim."

"Decided to take sides, did you? I suppose if Richard had the upper hand, you'd be offering him your services."

"Not at all. I never liked him. The sooner he's gone, the better, I say."

"Right. What's all this business about you being king?"

"Idle gossip. You know as well as I do that I'm not of the bloodline. Certain landowners made a joke about riding into London and crowning one of us king and before anyone knew it, people were passing it around as though it were fact. How my name got attached to it, I haven't a clue."

Henry looks over Fox for a moment. "Oh all right, I suppose we can use you. I guess you'll want some land in exchange for this, will you?"

"Why discuss such trivial details on such an important day? There's plenty of time to talk about who'll end up with one of several large patches of land situated in and around Yorkshire."

Henry shakes his head. "Fall in."

Charles and his men join the main body.

As they move along, Henry says to one of his commanders, "Is it just me or did Fox's standard bearer look a bit feminine to you?"

"Ah yes," the commander says, "rather sad story there. Turns out that as a child he was a high tenor in a boys' choir and his parents had him castrated to preserve the tone of his voice."

"That's horrible," Henry says.

As the battle wanes, the opposing forces break up into smaller groups, either trying to rally for another attack or fleeing for their lives. Charles is stationed on the road leading toward the shires of York and Lancaster, by which people can also make a break for Scotland. Whenever someone approaches him, Charles commands them to halt. "Friend or foe?"

"How do you distinguish one from another?"

"If you're here to fight then you're a foe. If you just want to run away then I say, be on your way my friend."

Charles spies a wagon moving along at a quick pace. He signals for the driver to stop and finds that it's a young man and woman, wearing white roses on their garments, with a wagon full of household items and other supplies.

"And who might you be?" Charles says to the driver.

"I'm Francis Tremaine and this is my sister Bethany. We're travelers headed toward Edinburgh."

Charles looks them over. "I doubt you'll get very far with those white roses on your clothes. I'd suggest you either rip them off or cover them. Pride be damned. If a Lancastrian mob catches sight of you, those roses will turn red quickly enough. You should err on the side of getting your sister to safety my friend."

Francis nods. He reaches into the back of the wagon and removes a cape which Bethany drapes around her shoulders. Then he rips the rose from his lapel.

"What's waiting for you in Edinburgh?"

"Distant family," Bethany says. "And friends who can help us start over."

Charles nods. "I suppose it's not a very good time to be a Yorkist around these parts."

"The sad part is I never once wielded a sword on their behalf," Francis says. "Our father was a supporter of Richard Plantagenet and pledged his loyalty."

"Not a totally bad proposition," Charles says. "He had as valid a claim as anyone."

"True, but once our father died, Bethany and I should have kept a low profile until the stronger side emerged."

"A lesson for the future, perhaps." Charles looks to several of his men. "Davies, Mackey, Seaborne. Round up about a dozen men and bring them here quickly."

The men do as Charles instructs.

"Now as much as I'd like to think a brother and sister of noble birth won't be harassed, I'm more of a realist."

When the men return Charles gives them instructions. "You are to accompany these good people until they're safely in Scottish territory. Then return to our manor as quickly as possible."

Charles rides over and removes a leather pouch from his side. He takes out a coin. "Hold out your hand."

Francis complies and Charles drops a weathered coin into his hand. Francis examines it to see it's a Roman coin bearing the likeness of Constantine.

"If anyone troubles you, show them that and tell them you're under the protection of Charles Fox. Anyone who wishes to make an issue of it, including Henry, can press the matter with me."

Francis nods. "You've been a true gentleman. I hope that one day we can repay your kindness."

"Perhaps. Now I suggest you go before you lose your light."

It has been many months since Isabella came to live in Bergeron's castle and in that time, they've become intimately involved and Isabella is several months pregnant. Bergeron reigned in his marauding activities and kept his promise to leave the convent alone. Isabella hasn't mentioned it, nor has she indicated any desire to keep up with their progress or return to them.

At first, she occupied a room in the north wing of the castle, and each day, she and Bergeron would dine together and occasionally walk around the grounds together. Their conversations were initially sparse and tentative, neither wanting to reveal much about themselves to the other. Eventually, though, he began to share more about his family.

"I probably had the closest bond with my youngest sister, Miranda. I called her Rani."

"How many years separated you?"

"Quite a few. I was in the army by the time she was born. My father remarried within a year of my mother's death. Rani's mother was his third wife."

Isabella expanded on the myth she developed about her upbringing. "I wish I had more memories of my parents. I was very young when they sent me to the convent."

"Do you recall how they looked?"

"I'm honestly not certain if the people I remember were them or someone else. There were lots of servants who looked after me. I do recall lots of laughter around our home. When they were present, I felt safe."

At dinner one evening, Isabella told Bergeron, "I am open to a visit after dinner, if you're in the mood."

"Really?"

"Absolutely. I don't need an answer now. You know how to find me."

"We'll see."

After Bergeron visited her rooms for several days, she moved into the master bedroom with him. It wasn't long before she realized she was pregnant. Bergeron was pleased by the news.

"I can only imagine how long our offspring will live."

One evening at dinner, a servant enters and whispers something to Bergeron.

"Is there?" He starts to rise. "If you will excuse me a moment my dear."

"What is it?"

"Nothing you need worry about. I'll handle it."

She claps her hand on the table and leans toward him. "Tell me."

"There's a contingent from the convent, no doubt here to try to win you back."

Isabella rises. "Let me speak to them."

"I don't think that's a good idea."

She goes to Bergeron and grasps his hand. "Are you afraid they'll succeed?" She touches her stomach. "Have I not demonstrated my loyalty to you?"

"Yes you have, admirably."

"Then they need to know where my allegiance lies. It's best they hear it from me."

Bergeron gives a slight bow. "By all means."

Isabella puts on her cape and descends to the vestibule. She nods to the servant at the door, who opens it for her. Outside, are eight nuns, led by Sister Marie.

"Oh. Belle. It's good to see you again."

"What do you want? Speak quickly. My time is limited."

Sister Marie wrings her hands. "We're here to check on you. We miss you terribly."

"Do you?" She looks around at the faces of the Sisters. "Well, you needn't bother with me any longer. I have found my place here."

"Please. If we could meet with you away from this place."

Isabella directs her eyes to a man standing to the rear of the entourage wearing a hood. He briefly raises his head and makes eye contact with her. She laughs and moves toward him.

"Is this your champion? The man you've brought with you to make sure I leave here?" She looks him over then suddenly produces a knife and plunges it into his chest. The man cries out, then crumples to the ground. The rest of the entourage reacts with horror. Isabella turns to Sister Marie and points the bloody knife at her.

"Take him back to your Mother Superior. Tell her this is my answer."

"Oh. Belle. No." Tears stream down Marie's face.

"Leave now!" Isabella takes a step toward Marie. "Before I lose my patience with you. Do not return."

Isabella goes back inside as the Sisters lift the man's body and place it onto their cart.

Bergeron greets her with applause. "Very effective. I should never have doubted you."

"Let's keep it that way." Isabella gives him a kiss.

Charles enters the Montgomery Trust building and asks to see Henry Owens. At the third floor reception area, he's instructed to wait and a few minutes later, a well-dressed Black man, appears.

"Mr. Fox?"

"Mr. Owens." Charles shakes his hand. He is escorted to Henry's desk.

"You said on the phone that you were referred by Victoria Wells."

"Yes, I'm an old friend of Victoria's. I have some funds I need to transfer from my bank in England. She suggested you might be able to assist me."

"An old friend." Henry looks around to be sure no one's listening then leans across his desk. "How old?"

"Yes, she said you knew." Fox leans forward and speaks in a low voice. "Give or take a few years, sixteen hundred and ninety-five."

"Whoa!" Henry says loudly then catches himself. "Sorry. I'm still getting used to, well, the other situation."

"I understand perfectly," Charles says. "Oh, and my wife has some funds she'd like to transfer from her bank in Paris, but I'll let her come in and give you the details."

"Your wife," Henry says. "Is she—?"

Charles holds up one finger, followed by four fingers, followed by seven fingers then two. Henry sighs and runs his hand over his forehead.

"Dad said learn accounting. It's just numbers." Henry takes out a form. "How much money are we talking about?"

"Here's my most recent statement, just so you know I'm not exaggerating." Charles hands his statement to Henry. "Oh and that's in pounds."

Henry's eyes widen. "You've got to be kidding. We have corporations that can't move this kind of money. Where did it all come from if you don't mind my asking?"

Charles leans forward. "Do you have any idea how much you can accrue when you have hundreds of years in which to do it?"

"No, but I appear to be learning." Henry holds up a finger. "Excuse me a moment."

He picks up his phone and dials an extension.

"Mr. Ferguson. Do you have a few minutes? There's someone I think you'll want to meet."

As they're disembarking in Sydney, Roland finds himself walking beside a pretty, petite, dark-haired woman with a pleasant smile and a bounce in her step. She's humming to herself.

"You're far too happy to be here, Miss."

"Pardon? Oh, I'm just glad to be away from London."

"I understand the sentiment. The name's Roland Fox."

"Pleased to meet you, Mr. Fox. I'm Amanda Seely."

"So what did you do Miss Seely?"

She giggles. "I got caught picking pockets."

"Obviously you weren't very good at it."

"Obviously." She mocks his inflection. "What did you do?"

"Turns out these gents had all this money they didn't need for anything. So I figured I'd put it to good use for 'em. Needless to say, they weren't too happy about it."

Amanda laughs again. "I imagine not. So, I guess we're just two hardened criminals, eh?"

Roland laughs.

"Have any idea where they're putting you to work?" Roland says.

"Not really. I heard them mention a household in the Northeastern part of town. Don't recall the family name."

"What a stroke of luck. I'm working in that same general area. Road work I believe. Maybe I'll catch sight of you once in a while."

"Maybe you will."

Behind them, a tall, thin man yells out, "Rolly! Thought you was waiting for me."

"Waiting for you? I found more pleasant company."

The thin man catches up to them. "Hello, Miss."

"Johnny Baynes, this is Amanda Seely," Roland says. "She says she'll be working over in the area we're going to be."

"Good for us," Johnny says. "I was worried about the scenery."

The three of them laugh.

"I'd shake your hand, Miss Seely, but unfortunately I haven't figured out how to get out of these irons," Johnny says.

"I'd wager if anyone could it'd be Johnny here," Roland says to Amanda. "The man's a mechanical genius."

"That what got you sent down here is it? Not enough mechanical geniuses?"

"No, that would have been the breaking and entering charge at my local blacksmith's. I commissioned him to forge some parts for me for this machine I was making, and he closed up early one night. I figured since I'd already paid him, I could just go in there and get my things. Police didn't see it that way."

"You got sent down on a first offense?"

"Well that was my first breaking and entering, but there had been some complaints by the neighbors about me being a nuisance, plus there was that small matter of the explosion."

"What explosion?"

"Johnny here was working the kinks out of one of his devices," Roland says. "Couldn't tell you what it was supposed to do, just that it was steam powered. Pressure valves became clogged and boom!"

"What was it supposed to do, Mr. Baynes?"

"Dig. It was a steam powered trench digger. Do the work of a whole crew of men in less than an hour."

As they arrive at the workstation, the men are separated from the women. Amanda waves to Roland and Johnny as she walks away.

"See there, Rolly. Things won't be so bad after all."

Half an hour after speaking to her parents, Katie is walking along a street in Aldgate in an old dress with her hair braided when Sally McIntyre comes up behind her. Sally is around five and a half feet and not more than a hundred pounds. She has honey-blonde hair and two different colored eyes. She stops and regards Katie angrily. "Hey!" Katie ignores her and keeps walking. Sally starts after her. "Hey, you, I thought I told you to stay out of my territory."

Katie turns, nonchalantly and replies with a thick Cockney accent. "Oh, Sally, you talking to me? I didn't hear you."

Sally gets into Katie's face. "You better hear me. You ain't getting no more warnings."

"Or what? Seems you're more talk than anything else."

Sally snaps out a dagger and holds it up to Katie's throat. "Talk about this, love."

Katie hesitates then laughs. "Pretty good with a dagger, ain't you? But how are you with your fists?"

"I'd sweep the streets with a scrawny bitch like you, I would."

"Behind the Bristol Pub in twenty minutes. I'll show you what this scrawny bitch can do."

When Katie arrives at the alley behind the Bristol Pub, there's already a crowd there. To one side a man is taking bets on who will win. The odds are clearly against Katie. She bets five pence in her favor then an equal amount on Sally. She wades through the crowd to find Sally already there, waiting with her sleeves pulled up and hair pinned back. Katie advances toward her.

"We gettin' started now or waiting for the crowd to get bigger?" Katie has a slight lilt in her voice.

"Just get to it. They'll show up."

The crowd starts chanting. "Fight, fight!"

Sally screams and rushes Katie holding her arms in front of her. Katie sidesteps and elbows Sally as she passes. Sally falls then kicks one of Katie's legs out from under her, knocking her down. The two begin wrestling, with a lot of hair pulling and punches. When they get to their feet again, Sally has a cut on her forehead and Katie has several scratches and scrapes on one side of her face and her dress is ripped.

This time she's the aggressor, leaping at Sally and throwing a series of punches to her midsection that doubles Sally over. Katie continues throwing punches until Sally grabs one of Katie's legs and again knocks her down. She begins kicking Katie in the side until Katie rolls away and starts to get to her feet. Sally rushes over to kick her again and Katie grabs Sally's foot and violently jerks it up causing Sally to crash onto the pavement. This leads to another session of violent tussling as they roll around trying to punch or avoid being punched.

Seventeen or eighteen minutes into the fight, both are pretty well bloodied up. They agree to take a ten minute rest and while they do two other women get up and fight in their place. Finished with their rest, they resume by exchanging a series of punches to the midsection and face. By this point, the "fight" has settled down into a vicious tussle, neither wanting to continue nor concede.

After several more rounds, in which the two get a little more banged up, they find themselves staring at one another diagonally across the alley with the onlookers chanting, "Fight, fight," but with far less conviction than before.

At last, Sally relaxes and gives Katie a crooked grin. "Ain't many what can go toe to toe with me and keep standin'."

Katie spreads her hands before her, palms up. "Call it a draw and I'll buy you a drink."

The crowd takes up a new chant: "Drink, drink."

In a great deal of pain, Sally walks over to Katie, who's also hurting, and throws her arm around Katie's shoulder and they head into the pub.

When Katie arrives home that evening still with a few cuts and bruises from the fight, Renee catches sight of her and exclaims, "Katherine Fox, what the hell have you been doing?"

Katie shrugs. "Believe me, it looked a lot worse an hour ago."

"Is this from that Sally person you didn't want us talking to?"

"One and the same."

Renee shakes her finger at Katie. "Well I hope this settles things."

Katie hugs her mother. "I'm sure it does."

Following her dustup with Sally, Katie decides to take an offer to perform in Vienna and readies herself to leave England. As she's waiting for her carriage in front of the house, a familiar voice comes from beside her. "'Scuse me, miss, might I have a word?"

Hesitantly, Katie turns to see Sally McIntyre there. Sally's eyes widen when she realizes who she's addressing. "You!"

"Hello Sally," Katie says, not even remotely trying to disguise her voice. "Fancy meeting you here."

"You're some kind of society woman, you is. You tellin' me I got me arse handed to me by some society woman?"

"I'm an actress. I go down to the East End to learn the vernacular."

"Vernacu—" Sally says, quizzically.

"How people talk. It helps me with my acting."

"I never knew. Guess you must be pretty good."

"The critics don't always agree," Katie says with a chuckle. Sally's expression tells Katie she doesn't get the joke. "I do my best."

"And what happened to your face?" Sally leans in to examine Katie more closely. "I'm still all cut and bruised up and you look like you wasn't even there."

"What can I say, I heal quickly. What was it you wanted to ask before you found out it was me?"

"I was going to ask for money for the orphans, but seeing as how it's you, you probably know it ain't."

Katie smiles. "What is the usual donation, miss?"

It takes Sally a moment to figure out what Katie's asking. Then she gets back into character. "Oh, well, usually a person might give a few shillings. These orphans, you see, they ain't got nobody else."

"I see." She takes out her purse and removes several bills and hands them to Sally.

"Blimey, ma'am," Sally says with a smile. "We can feed a lot of orphans with this."

As they speak Katie's carriage arrives. Sally looks over it, greatly impressed.

"It'll be a cold day in 'ell before I ever get to ride in one of those."

"Then it must be freezing." Katie tosses her head toward the carriage. "Hop in. I'll drop you at the docks." Sally hesitates. Katie places her hand on Sally's shoulder. "Come on, you can tell everyone you really fleeced this sucker."

Sally grins then boards, followed by Katie.

"Incredible," Ferguson says upon being introduced to Charles. "Victoria Wells said that there were others like her, but I never imagined I'd meet another one."

"Vickie's a great kid," Charles says. "She made it through some tough times and came out the better for it."

Henry chuckles. "It's funny you call her a kid."

"To me she is. I guess it's a matter of perspective."

"So you were born during the Roman Empire?" Ferguson says.

"Toward the end. I figured I must have been born just before or just after Constantine became emperor."

"How do you figure that?" Ferguson says.

"When I was a very young man, the men of my tribe would occasionally engage Roman legions in battle. They were almost always carrying coins embossed with Constantine's likeness." He raises his finger and continues, "In fact, I have some with me if you'd like to take a look." He produces a small, worn leather bag secured with a drawstring, opens it, and takes out two heavily worn grey-green coins and hands one each to Ferguson and Henry.

"They've held up better than I thought they would," he says.

"Amazing," Henry says to which Ferguson nods.

"Of course, I can't be more exact on my date of birth than that. We weren't on the Julian or Gregorian calendar. I believe we marked time via phases of the moon, but I forget exactly how it worked. The women tended to keep track of the passage of time while the men went out hunting and attacking Romans."

Ferguson starts to hand the coin back but Fox waves it off.

"You sure?" Ferguson says.

"Where could I spend it?" Fox says with a sly grin on his face. He motions to Henry to keep his as well.

"Now as Henry has already noted, it will be difficult to move this amount of money all at once," Ferguson says. "Otherwise, we'd raise a heck of a lot of red flags from ATF to Homeland Security to the IRS."

Henry concurs. "But maybe we can transfer some of it

to our firm, and some to our various associates with an eye toward transferring it here later." He leans forward resting his elbows on his knees and concludes, "But even then, it's going to take a several months to get it all over here."

Charles bobs his head back and forth a time or two as he thinks it over. He gives them a shrug. "I've got time."

When they arrive back at the convent, Sister Marie dispatches two of the sisters to inform the Mother Superior of Belle's response to their visit. She has the others place the man's body in a downstairs chamber where he can be prepared for burial. While awaiting instructions, Marie makes a list of the items that will be needed to prepare him for the catacombs. Before gathering them, she makes the sign of the cross and bows her head.

Several moments pass before a commotion causes her to lift her eyes and when she does, she is startled to see the man's hands shaking. She springs from her seat as his body begins to convulse and he takes in a gasp of air then sits up.

"Saints preserve us!" She grasps her rosary, holding the cross in front of her.

"Where am I?" The man looks at Sister Marie who watches him in fright. "I'm pretty sure you're not supposed to be here."

"What manner of being are you?"

"That's rather hard to explain."

The Mother Superior enters, exasperated.

"Marie, what is the meaning of this? My instructions were that no one was to remain with this man." She turns to him. "How are you feeling?"

He rubs his chest. "Reasonably well, all things considered."

"Mother, I meant no offense. I was praying for him. But I've just witnessed the most miraculous thing."

"Yes, I suppose it would seem as such. Marie, it is vital that you do not tell anyone what you've witnessed here. Everyone must continue to believe this man is dead."

"I don't understand."

The man rises as the Mother Superior presents him. "This is Nathaniel Fox, Belle's brother."

"Brother?"

Nathaniel bows. "At your service."

"Then you're as old as Belle," Marie says.

"I most certainly am not. She's at least fifty years my senior. But we do share that attribute."

The Mother Superior explains. "It was important we let Belle know Nathaniel arrived, but we couldn't risk having Lord Bergeron find out about it. He has spies everywhere so it's difficult to know who to trust, even here in the convent."

"Yes, I understand. Then you both can conquer death?"

"To some extent," Nathaniel says.

"And, as you might imagine, it's vital no one knows about that as well," the Mother Superior tells Marie.

"Of course."

The Mother Superior checks the door. "It is fortuitous that you're here, Marie. I know I can trust you. I'll need you to assist Nathaniel, since he can't risk being seen."

"I'll do whatever's required of me, Mother. I'm so happy to know that you're well, sir and that Isabella has not turned away from us."

Nathaniel concurs. "You and me both." He turns to the Mother Superior. "Now, I strongly advise you to get packed. I have a contingent of men awaiting my signal to escort you."

"We are already collecting what we'll need and will be prepared in a matter of days. How will you get word to your sister?"

He gives her a wink. "Oh. I'll think of something."

After their sentences are lifted, Roland, Johnny and Amanda settle in Perth, as Johnny has secured an engineering job there. The three are practically inseparable, but as time goes on, it becomes apparent that Johnny and Amanda are falling in love. This troubles Roland because he's in love with Amanda as well. Because of their differences, though, he has never told her and he's not sure what would happen if he did.

He knows that Amanda cares for him, but she's never expressed any desire for them to be more than friends. As his love for her grows, though, Roland realizes that friendship is no longer enough for him.

Before he can determine what to do about it, Johnny corners Roland in the pub.

"Rollie, you're the first person I'm telling about this, so keep it to yourself, okay."

"Okay, whatever it is."

"I'm asking Mandy to marry me tonight."

Roland feels a grinding in the pit of his stomach.

"Great news, Johnny! You two will make the perfect couple."

"Hey, I am fully expecting you to be my best man."

"I'd be insulted if you didn't ask."

As the wedding day approaches, Roland wrestles with his feelings for Amanda versus his friendship with Johnny. He tells himself: "If I can't be with her, I'll be happy for her and Johnny."

This does not make it any easier to watch them get married, particularly since he'll be front and center throughout.

On the day of the wedding, Roland dutifully arrives at the church an hour before the ceremony. Johnny's there, anxious over what's about to happen.

"Rolly tell me this is all true. I'm really getting married. Would you have ever thought it while we were making our rounds back in London?"

"Never in a million years. I envy you. She's a great girl. You two will be very happy together."

"I'm glad you could be here. It just wouldn't be right for me to take this big of a step without you at my side." He gives Roland a hug. "You're the best friend a man could have."

"No, you are."

"Say, I've sprung for a photographer all day. "Capture every minute of this, eh?"

"Great. Something to show the kids."

"Kids? Oh, god, it's really happening isn't it?"

"It sure is."

The ceremony is short and to the point. Johnny and Amanda exchange their vows then the rings. After their first kiss, they invite everyone to a local park for the reception.

Amanda sees Roland hanging around in the crowd and pulls him aside.

"Roland, I am so glad you could be here for Johnny and for me. Just think, I'm an old married lady now."

"You'll never be old. You made a beautiful bride."

She gives him a hug.

"You have always been such a good friend. You made coming here a lot of fun. I don't know what I'd have done if I hadn't had you and Johnny around all that time."

"It wouldn't have been nearly as pleasant without you either."

Johnny summons them both for a group portrait then he and Roland pose for a shot.

Roland sticks around until nearly the end of the festivities then decides he has to go. He finds Johnny and Amanda.

"I just want to say again to you two, congratulations. I know you're going to have a wonderful life together."

"Hey, there Rolly, you're going to be a part of it too. Where would I be without my best friend?"

"Certainly. But I have to head home now. I've got a job waiting for me in Sydney."

"Sydney?" Amanda says. "Doing what?"

"Construction. It's temporary but could become permanent."

"What's all this?" Johnny says. "Why didn't you tell me about this job? If it's construction you want, we're going to have all you can handle before long."

"Oh don't worry. I'll stay in touch, and you can be sure anytime I'm off I'll be right here."

"Sure thing," Johnny says.

"Yes, Roland, please do stay in touch and I want to see you on a regular basis," Amanda says.

"Guys, I'm just going to Sydney, I'm not heading back

to London. I'll get back here every chance I get."

First Johnny then Amanda gives him a hug then he's off.

"Goodbye Johnny, Mandy."

For the first few months, Roland writes to Johnny and Amanda and makes it back for a visit or two. As time goes on, the letters and visits become less frequent until they stop altogether. Johnny and Amanda wonder what happened to their friend, but their kids and his job take up most of their time. Before they realize it, many years have gone by without a word from Roland.

Renee and Charles have been in Paris less than two hours when they receive an urgent request to perform at a benefit for the Danse du Monde troupe later that evening.

Renee regards Charles with her hands on her hips. "We barely have time to unpack, not to mention figure out our wardrobe."

"Or what we'll perform, though I suppose we could just trot out our last continental act."

"What exactly is our incentive for saying yes?"

"Ah. The best incentive. We finally have a chance to watch Gisele Bourgeois dance."

"You think they'll let us add that as a condition of employment?"

"They will if we refuse to perform otherwise."

The Foxes know Gisele as a rising star in the Parisian dance scene, said to combine grace with athleticism in a style which has been praised for both its power and beauty.

When they arrive at the theater, Renee outlines their conditions for employment.

"We wish to see the performance beforehand. If the entire performance is too long to allow us adequate preparation, we are willing to limit our attendance to when Gisele Bourgeois is onstage."

The theater owner throws up his hands. "No, no, that's quite out of the question. You hardly have any time to prepare as it is."

Renee shakes her head. "Oh, dear. I just remembered we have another engagement tonight that takes precedence over this one."

"You're kidding. Why are you only now thinking of this?"

"We're very busy and the request came so suddenly, I didn't have time to check."

The owner relents. "All right. I'll make it part of your agreement that you can see the show."

"You're mistaken, darling." Charles gives her an approving grin. "I know which engagement you're thinking of and it's next week."

"Ah! My mistake."

As the ballet commences they find themselves seated near the rear of the theater.

"She is exquisite," Renee whispers to Charles. "The critics don't do her justice."

"They don't. It's like she's floating across the floor."

Charles lets his eyes wander across the audience. He stops when he spots a familiar face, one he never imagined he would see here and leans toward Renee. "Renee. Third row, toward the middle. Is that who I think it is?"

Renee looks. "It's Bergeron."

"What's he doing here?" As they watch, Bergeron leans toward a small, redheaded woman beside him and says something. The woman glances at him and nods with an excited smile on her face. "Is that his daughter?"

"Another one?"

A bearded man behind them leans forward and speaks in a hushed tone. "Could you please be quiet?"

Charles looks back at him. "You be quiet. We're trying to watch the show if you don't mind."

The man sits back then makes an obscene gesture which Charles finds amusing.

Gisele is on stage for ten or twelve more minutes, after which Renee and Charles rise, exit, and head downstairs to the ballroom.

"Do you want the English or French part first?" Charles says.

"I'll start with the French," Renee replies. "Then we can switch after 'crown heads of Europe'."

"I thought we switched after 'known throughout the land'?"

"No, we changed, remember? To keep us on our toes."

"Or flat on our faces."

When they reach the ballroom, Charles and Renee walk the floor, examining it for imperfections that might cause problems during their dance routine. Once they've checked out the area where they'll be performing, Charles takes Renee in his arms and they do several turns around the floor with a waltz. They circle once then stop and Charles releases Renee who steps away from him while holding his left hand and once they're standing beside one another, Charles bows while Renee curtseys. "Good?"

She nods. "Yes, but let's take it one more time, entering from the other side. You never know where the dignitaries will congregate."

They try it again as she suggests.

"Works for me," Renee says.

"Great." Thunderous applause erupts from above. "Let's go raid the hors d'oeuvres before the crowd gets here."

"Good idea." Renee rubs her hands in front of her. "I'll race you."

They both jog over to the table with Renee slightly ahead. When she reaches the table first, she throws up both arms and does a brief impromptu dance.

They eat a plate or two as the first of the guests arrive. Seeing Bergeron and his companion, Charles says, "Now we can get to the bottom of this."

He puts his arm around Renee, and they head toward Bergeron, who sees them and seems less than thrilled.

"Bergeron don't tell me it's that time of the century again," Charles says.

"Can't we make it through at least a hundred year span without the pattern repeating?" Renee says.

They are introduced to the young woman, named Victoria, who Bergeron introduces as his protégé. They speak for several minutes before Renee takes Victoria's arm. "Hey boys, I'm going to steal away with Victoria, so, we can get to know one another."

Charles stays behind with Bergeron.

"Your protégé," Charles says. "Trying a different tack this time, are you?"

"Yes, my protégé. I'm certain Victoria is capable of having a bright future, given the right direction."

A waiter comes by with champagne. Bergeron takes one, but Charles waves him off. "None for me. I'm performing. Seriously, Bergeron, it has been nearly a millennium since you gave a whit about helping anyone — even someone like us."

"I can't describe it. The thought of being able to influence someone just starting out on that very, very long road just seemed appealing."

"I understand the sentiment, just not from you."

Bergeron looks around at the crowd.

"Think about it, Fox. All those years we spent clawing around in darkness. Could you imagine how it would have been if only we had someone to guide us?"

Charles' response is interrupted by a burst of applause near the door, and he turns to see the dancers entering.

"Excuse me. There's someone I need to speak to."

He steps over to Gisele and addresses her in French. "Miss Bourgeois? I'm Charles Fox. My wife Renee and I will be performing tonight."

"Yes Mr. Fox."

"I just wanted to say how totally captivating Renee and I found your performance. We both agree that the critics don't do you justice."

"You're very kind. Your name is Fox? I believe we are working together in a show a few weeks from now, are we not?"

"We are in that show, and I'm pleased to hear you are."

Their conversation is interrupted by the theater owner who pulls Gisele away to introduce her to a patron. After a few pleasantries, Gisele steps away and focuses on something across the room. Charles looks to see Victoria approaching Gisele. At that same moment, Renee grabs his arm. "We've got to get ready."

"Sure." Charles puts his arm around her, and they walk quickly to the side of the room. They pass two patrons who motion toward Gisele, and one says, "Yes, it is her!"

"What did you find out about Victoria?" Charles says.

"For one thing she's desperately smitten with Gisele Bourgeois."

"True, but so is most of Paris. I saw her headed over to talk to Gisele before you came along."

"Looks like she didn't make it."

Charles looks to see Victoria standing alone across the room. Bergeron is nowhere to be seen.

"I gave her our card. Victoria passed the test."

"Really? I want a full accounting when we're done here."

The master of ceremonies takes the floor to announce them. Charles takes Renee in his arms in a waltz position.

"Break a leg," Renee says to him.

"And a couple of ribs, too."

The master of ceremonies says, "Bienvenue s'il vous plaît Carlton et Carlotta!" and Charles says to Renee, "Here we go. One and a two—."

Isabella puts on her cape and exits onto the grounds of the castle. She sets out into the forest for a long walk as is her custom when Bergeron is away attending to business. As she approaches the clearing near a large pond, she notes a figure seated on a rock, staring at the water.

"You, there. Are you supposed to be here?"

"Thanks to you, I'm not supposed to be anywhere." The voice is unmistakably that of her brother. He turns to face her.

"Good to see you again. How are you feeling?"

"I don't like taking a knife to the chest, but since it was in service to a good cause, I'll get over it."

"Glad to hear it. I trust you've brought news."

"I have indeed." He pats the rock beside him, and Isabella sits. "You wouldn't recognize your old home. It's a shell of its former self."

"So, the Sisters are away?"

"Yes. The last report was that they're within a day of their destination. Of course, to outside observers, everything looks normal. The fires are still burning. The linens are hanging on the lines."

"Wonderful. Then all that's left is for me to make my escape."

"Any idea how you'll pull that off?"

"I'll need to occupy Bergeron with something else. You say the convent still looks lived in?"

"Yes. And it will continue to do so until the few men I left there leave."

"Good. That should provide enough of a diversion. When Bergeron returns day after tomorrow, I'll make it known I simply can't live with it there as a reminder."

"I'll inform my men to be away by daybreak."

Isabella starts to rise and hesitates, considering whether she should reveal her condition to Nathaniel.

"Is there something else on your mind?"

She decides against it for the time being. "No. It can wait."

A few nights later, at dinner, Isabella seems restless and unfocused. Bergeron takes note.

"Is something wrong?"

"It's the Sisters. I received a note while you were away imploring me to meet with them."

"Why didn't you mention it when I returned?"

"I burned it. I didn't want to trouble you with it. But, as it turns out, I'm very troubled by it. You know I severed ties to them."

"Yes. That was quite obvious."

"If only they weren't there as a constant reminder."

"I have only stayed away because of our agreement."

"That's true. In that case, I rescind that agreement."

"Are you saying what I think you are?"

"I am. I want to be rid of them once and for all."

"It pleases me to hear you say that. I would be lying if I told you I was happy with their continued existence."

"Good. Then let me be as explicit as possible. I don't just want you to take care of it. I want to witness it."

"You've changed quite a bit since you've been here. I

never thought I'd hear these words from you."

"I have a new life. A new future, thanks to you. It's best to sever all ties to the past."

"I fully agree. Tomorrow, I'll assemble my forces, and we'll strike at dawn the following day."

"I can't wait."

The Foxes are informed that several of the Jewish families that live near their villa in Castile have been picked up by the Inquisition. They book passage to the kingdom and request an audience with Tomás de Torquemada, the Grand Inquisitor.

"We're here about the Jewish families your people intercepted in Castile," Charles says.

"What is your concern with them?" Torquemada says.

"Their family has served ours for many years," Charles says. "They're reliable and trustworthy and have done no harm to anyone."

"We determine what harm they've done," Torquemada says.

"What could they possibly tell you that you don't already know?" Renee says.

Without acknowledging or even facing her, Torquemada addresses Charles. "You should train your woman to have more respect."

Charles takes a step forward. "You will not speak of my wife in that manner."

"I speak with the authority of the Church."

Renee pulls him away before the situation goes any further. "Charles, this man is an idiot," she says in a low voice. "Let's call on Ferdinand and Isabella. They have much more sway here."

As they're heading back to their carriage, Charles spots a familiar face and goes over.

"Bergeron. What are you doing here?"

"I work here. Who's your friend?"

"My wife, Renee. She's one of us."

"Is she? You're a very lucky man."

"You work here?" Charles says. "Doing what?"

"The Inquisition needed someone with a certain type of expertise to help with their interrogations."

"In other words, torture," Renee says. "How could you even consider such an assignment? These people aren't like us. When they die they stay dead."

"What's that to me? They need my knowledge and are willing to pay top dollar. Who am I to tell them how to use it."

"Who are you to tell them anything?" Charles says. "No one's forcing you."

"Let's just say we have a philosophical disagreement and leave it at that."

"Do you have any pull with them?" Charles says. "We're trying to get a couple of families released."

"Who are they?"

"One is the family of Aaron bar Tevya," Renee says. "And the other is the family of Abraham ben Joseph."

"Aaron bar Tevya was fine last I heard. Abraham ben Joseph didn't make it, I'm afraid."

"What do you mean by that?" Charles says. "Surely they didn't torture him. The man was seventy years old."

"I'm not sure the Inquisitors took that into account. As far as I know, his family is well, but they aren't really my concern."

"These are human beings," Charles says. "Just because they don't live as long as we do, that's no reason to treat them differently."

"Again, let's call it a philosophical disagreement. Still, I'll see what I can do. I can't promise anything."

Not quite an hour later, Bergeron returns with an older man, two older women and several young adults and children. They hurry to where the Foxes are.

"Aaron," Charles says to the older man. "Are you all right?"

"My family is fine, but poor Abraham is dead. We just want to get out of here."

Charles thanks Bergeron then returns to the group. One of the women points to Bergeron as he walks away. "That man was there when Abraham died."

"He was?" Renee says. "What was he doing?"

"Watching, and directing the Inquisitors."

"He's an acquaintance and nothing more," Renee says. "Let's get you out of here before something changes."

Charles asks, "What happened to Abraham's body?"

The woman has tears in her eyes. "They burned it."

Charles shakes his head.

"We've made arrangements for you to go to Amsterdam," Renee says. "They're more tolerant there for now. Once things cool down, we can bring you back or find other accommodations."

"Thank you both," Aaron says. "We won't forget your kindness."

"Let's just get you to safety," Charles says.

Nathaniel waits on a ridge overlooking the valley, where he and Isabella agreed to meet as soon as she manages to get away from the castle. The sound of hoof beats causes him to turn and watch as Isabella rides up and stops beside him.

"Did you have any trouble getting away?"

"Not at all. Bergeron was totally obsessed with the sisters and didn't give me a second thought, as I anticipated. He did leave a guard, and I'm certain the poor man will soon be finding out the penalty for taking my suggestion of joining the fray instead of staying with me."

"You know he's going to look for you."

"All the clues I've been feeding him point to Saxony. Hopefully he won't be thinking of France. If he figures it out, well, that's why you're here."

"Say the word and I'll go and finish him off for you. Given the reports I've had of him from the convent, it would be my pleasure."

Isabella shakes her head.

"There's been too much bloodshed already. As much as I feel he deserves it, I don't want you to be a party to it. He'll answer for his crimes one day. There's something else you need to know."

"What's that?"

In response, she opens her cape to reveal her pregnancy.

"I'm not sure I expected that. Are you sure you want to bring his child into the world?"

"It will be my child, too. I don't know what horrors created that monster, but I'm certain I'll do all I can to shield this child from all that."

"I'm sure you will. I suppose he couldn't have been totally evil if he was able to win you over to such an extent."

"The life he leads can be very seductive. There were times when it was just us, that he could be the most gentle and caring person I've known."

"I suppose everyone has the capacity for good as well as evil. Even someone like him."

"His way of life is very tempting. Except, he's all alone. He doesn't have someone like you or our parents to provide support or counsel."

"It almost seems sad. How were you able to stay focused?"

"I taught myself a phrase: 'I became what I beheld.' Whenever I felt myself being drawn in too closely, I would recite it as a reminder to maintain focus."

"That was smart. Do you feel you had any effect on him?"

"Very little, if any. Bergeron's evil intentions were never far from the surface. Whatever has made him what he is lies deep within him. Nothing I could do would ever change that."

"If anyone could have, I'd have bet on you." He looks away and shakes his head. "Many changes ahead. But, the French manor can benefit from having a child around. I might not be the father, but I'll be one hell of an uncle."

Isabella laughs. "I have no doubt about that."

As they ride, Nathaniel has an insight.

"If all I've heard of him is true, I strongly suspect that Bergeron will surmise that Saxony was just a ruse. If I had to wager, I'd say he'll look for you in the region where the convent relocated."

"You may be right. Perhaps a further surprise should await him there."

"I was hoping you'd say that."

Katherine Fox has been back in London long enough that the Austrian accent she'd picked up while performing in and around Vienna for the better part of two decades has started to fade back to her customary English lilt. Since her parents are performing in England at the same time, she decided to continue using her Austrian stage name Katerina Fuchs. She accepted an audition immediately upon arrival.

"I have just concluded a run in a rather bittersweet drama in Vienna," she tells the director for whom she's auditioning. "A comedy would be a nice change of pace."

The director looks over his notes. "Is there anything you can do about your accent? I'm actually looking for an English girl for this part."

Katie considers it, then replies in an upper crust British cadence. "I don't understand. What accent do you mean?"

The director nods. "That will work."

Katherine lands the role of Florence Trenchard in the revival of a Tom Taylor comedy with an ironically tragic history.

While attending an opening night party with her cast mates, she meets Francis Stone and his sister Bethany, who both appear to be in their mid-twenties.

"Miss Fuchs, Francis and I very much enjoyed your performance."

"Thank you, Miss Stone. I'm never totally certain if the jokes are landing."

"Oh, I think you had a reasonable idea," Francis interjects. "Surely you heard the laughter. There was quite a bit as I recall."

"You're too kind, Mr. Stone. I may have taken note of some of it."

She finds them to be a fun pair and spends much of her time talking to one or the other at the party. She's especially drawn to Francis.

"Have you had an opportunity to work with Mr. Shaw?" Francis asks.

"George? A few near misses, but no, I haven't had the pleasure just yet."

"I understand he's giving a talk not far from our home.

Would you care to accompany me?"

"I would indeed. Thank you for the offer, Mr. Stone."

To prepare, Katie reads as many of Shaw's plays, pamphlets, and articles she can get her hands on. She isn't sure whether a relationship with Francis will develop from their mutual interest in one another, but she's excited over the possibility of getting to know him.

She's just auditioned for a newly written drama about the conditions in London's East End. In preparation, she once again took the opportunity to familiarize herself with conditions there from a firsthand perspective. Until earlier this week Katie has been splitting her time between her flat near the theater and a small room she shared with two other women, a middle-aged, nervous woman named Alice, and a younger woman named Vickie who Katherine rarely saw. In between, she roamed the streets, interacting with anyone who caught her interest, and observing how folks behaved.

While she tried to affect the guise of a desperate street person, she rarely ventured into Whitechapel after sundown. This had little to do with the Ripper killings. Thanks to her parents, Katie knows very well how to defend herself and wasn't planning on propositioning strange men in dark alleys in the first place. On some level, she even welcomed the opportunity to confront the perpetrator, since she's certain the outcome would be much different than for the other unfortunate souls who had encountered him.

When Katie arrives at the theater for the penultimate performance of her play, the stage manager greets her with a wide smile. "Seems you have quite an admirer out there."

"What do you mean?"

He leads her to the dressing room. "See for yourself."

Entering, she's first aware of several of the other women in the cast gathered around the tiny corner she's been using to get ready for a performance. It soon becomes apparent what's attracted their attention. Her entire section is filled with floral arrangements, leaving her little room to get ready.

"Who sent these?" Katie goes over and pulls the card from one, opens it, and reads: "Viel Glück, Frau Fuchs —B"

The stage manager narrows his eyes. "What does that mean?"

"Break a leg."

"Ooo," another actor says. "Who's this B?"

Katie considers it a few moments when suddenly she's startled by a voice from the door.

"Good morrow, Kate, for that's your name, I hear."

She turns and, from the description given to her by her parents and older sister, recognizes the man standing there. "Bergeron."

He advances toward her and her guard goes up.

"I do hope I wasn't too overzealous in my admiration. I just had to let you know I came to see your performance."

Without removing her eyes from him, Katie addresses the stage manager. "Are all these from him?"

The stage manager nods. "They all came from the same florist and arrived at the same time."

"Get rid of them."

"You mean just throw them out?"

"I don't care what you do with them. I want them out of here." She has a thought. "Wait." She wags her finger. "There's a mortuary just down the road. Please take all these and distribute them among the unfortunate souls there."

"Are you serious?"

"Do I look like I'm joking?"

The manager heaves a sigh. "I'll round up a few stage-hands."

One of the other women steps forward. "Hey Mr. B, if Katie doesn't want them maybe someone else would."

Katie puts up her hand. "Trust me when I say, you do not want anything from this man."

Bergeron chuckles. "Oh, well, what is it they say about the punishment for good deeds."

Katie crosses her arms. "Good deeds? What would you possibly know about good deeds?"

Bergeron throws up his hands in a shrug. "Maybe it's

the thought that counts after all." He turns. "I'll leave you for now, but I'll be anxiously awaiting your performance. Do be sure to give my regards to your sister and niece."

With that, he leaves.

The woman who stepped forward says, "What was that all about?"

"Bad blood. Very, very bad blood." Katie speaks to the boy who's moving the flowers onto a cart. "Anything more from 'B' goes straight to the funeral home."

"Yes ma'am."

She turns to the stage manager. "He does not get back here again. Do you hear me?"

"Absolutely."

"Most importantly keep an eye on the women in the cast and do not let him go near them, especially alone."

"Any particular reason?"

"He's extremely dangerous. That's all you need to know."

Throughout the night's performance, Katie can't ignore the thought that Bergeron is out there watching her. Rather than allowing it to distract her — which, she suspects, was the reason he made his presence known — she instead channels the anxiety into her performance. She imagines the character of Coyle, the main antagonist who's scheming for Florence's hand in marriage, is Bergeron and she reacts accordingly.

After the curtain calls and once she's finished removing her makeup and changing, Katherine checks backstage and in the concert hall to be sure Bergeron isn't still around. Finally, she says her goodbyes to the other actors and exits the rear door of the theater, looking all around her as she makes her way to the street.

Just as she's certain she's alone, she's startled by a woman's voice with a thick Cockney accent near her. "'Scuse me, Miss? Don't I know you?"

Katherine turns to see a small woman walking in her direction. The woman is elegantly dressed, which contradicts her distinct working-class accent. Katherine takes a few steps toward her and gets a good look at the woman's face. "Vickie? It is Vickie, right?"

"That's me — and I believe I know you as Plain Kate."

Katherine laughs a bit. "Yes, Plain Kate. I'm not her anymore. I've gone back to being just Kate, or Katerina to be precise." She looks Vickie over. "You appear to be doing rather well since the last time I saw you."

"I'm making it."

"How's Alice? I was hoping to speak to her before I left but she never came back to the flat."

"She's dead." Vickie has a slight catch in her voice.

Katherine covers her mouth. "Oh dear. She was such a sweet lady. Did you speak to her beforehand?"

Vickie shakes her head. "By the time I found her she was already gone. I was coming to let her know I had the rent money."

"Oh, I took care of the rent. I was planning on doing it anyway if no one else came up with any."

"Why didn't you just tell us?"

Katherine shrugs. "If I'd told you I could get it, you'd want to know where I got it, and I wasn't sure I'd have a convincing story."

Vickie runs her hand over her throat. Her voice takes on an edge.

"I always figured you wasn't from the streets. You was always too clean. Even dirty you was cleaner than everybody else I knew. Why would you want to live like that?"

"Acting for one thing. I spent several years in Moscow performing and they have some interesting ideas on how to approach a role. I'm playing a person from the streets in my next play, so I thought I'd see how people really live."

"People. Like me, eh? For your information, that's how we live. We ain't acting."

"I'm sorry. I didn't mean to insult you. I'm interested in people and rather than watch from a distance, I like to see life close up. I always enjoyed interacting with you and Alice, even though our encounters were rather brief."

Something occurs to Vickie, and she reaches into her purse. "Oh. I found this on your side of the room." She hands Katherine a Roman coin bearing the likeness of Constantine.

Katherine looks at it and smiles. "Thank you so much. I was afraid I'd lost it forever."

"Somebody told me what it is. Why do you have it?"

"My father gave one to me and each of my siblings and said that if we're ever in trouble and need his help, to send for him using that and he'll know it's from us."

"Glad I could get it back to you." She turns. "I got to go. I got someone waiting on me."

Kate waves to Vickie. "Thank you again and take care of yourself, Vickie."

Vickie waves as she moves off in the direction she came.

Kate heads back to her flat several blocks away and hurries to get out of her everyday clothing and into something more festive as she has a date with Francis and Bethany. Tonight she's meeting them for what Francis terms a surprise.

When they arrive to pick her up, Katherine is happy to see Bethany is accompanied by a gentleman who she introduces as Guy de Rolfe whose family is said to have come over with the Conqueror.

Katie recognizes the family name. "I've heard of him — Guy the Benevolent. He died in battle and insisted his lands be divided among his troops."

"You are well-versed in English lore, Miss Fuchs," de Rolf says.

Francis refuses to divulge what he has planned, only that it should be fun. Katherine is somewhat surprised when they show up at a music hall not far from the theater where she's performing. As they enter, Katherine is amused to see the marquee announcing the "internationally famous" couple Carlton and Carlotta, her parents in their latest stage incarnation.

"What?" Francis says with a grin. "Too lowbrow for a famous actress like you?"

"Not at all. I've seen this couple on the continent and they're very entertaining."

"Should be an enjoyable evening then. Bethany and I saw their show a few nights ago and Beth couldn't stop talking about them afterward and singing songs from their act."

Bergeron fumes as a servant enters and reluctantly approaches and bows before him.

"Where is she?"

"My Lord, she appears to have stolen away while you were engaged at the convent. She took nothing with her but the clothes she was wearing."

"Why was she not guarded as I ordered?"

"She appears to have dismissed the guard and sent him off to help with the assault."

"If he's still drawing breath within these premises, I want him locked up until I think of a suitable end for him."

"Yes, my Lord."

"Send riders in all directions. I want her trail found quickly."

"At once, my Lord."

The servant starts to leave but Bergeron stops him.

"Have someone also find out where the convent relocated. I wouldn't be a bit surprised to find her nearby."

"Yes, my Lord."

The servant exits.

"You may have saved your precious convent, but be assured, I will find you. Whatever your name is."

Bergeron's contacts in Saxony and throughout France do not prove to be helpful in locating Belle, but after many weeks, he finally receives a promising lead from the region near where the convent has gone and sets out to learn more on his own. When he arrives, after numerous inquiries over several days, he is, at last, directed to a man in rustic clothing who is said to have served the woman Bergeron seeks.

"Good morning sir. How may I be of service to you?"

"I've heard reports of a beautiful woman who lives in this region. Could you tell me where I can find her?"

"That may be a bit difficult, sir. This region is known for women of exceptional beauty."

"This woman is called Belle. She has a child and is said to be older than she seems."

"Ah, sir, then I know exactly who you mean — a woman known for her beauty as well as her exceptional virtue."

"That's debatable, but it sounds the way someone might describe her."

"Then I do know where to find her."

"Excellent! Tell me where she is, and I'll reward you handsomely." Bergeron produces a sack full of coins.

"I could tell you, but I won't, not for any amount."

"I don't believe I heard you properly."

"You heard me well enough — Bergeron." He draws a sword.

"I see." Bergeron swings a leg over his horse and drops to the ground. He draws his sword. "If you know my name, then you know my reputation."

"I fear neither your name, your reputation, nor your sword."

"Then you're a fool."

"You're not the first to tell me that. But we shall see."

They fight. Both are aggressive and neither is able to gain the upper hand. They separate and face off.

"Your reputation is well earned. We may be at this a while."

Bergeron laughs. "If you're going to do battle with me, at least tell me your name."

"Nathaniel."

"Then I'll make you a deal, Nathaniel. If you break off now, and let me go on my way, I'll not pursue you. You'll lose no honor."

"And if I continue?"

"You'll die."

Nathaniel laughs.

"Then I'll rise to fight again another day."

Bergeron looks him over with narrowed eyes.

"You're one of us?"

"We only have one attribute in common. Otherwise, we're nothing alike. Perhaps Belle failed to mention, she has a brother."

Bergeron shakes his head. "Why am I not surprised she lied about being an orphan?" He raises his sword. "Then you'll share equally in my wrath. You may be a long-timer, but we can be permanently killed."

"That's what I've heard."

Nathaniel readies himself and they square off again.

The battle becomes more heated with neither gaining the upper hand. At last, Bergeron swipes his sword at Nathaniel catching him just above his left hip. Nathaniel staggers backward then collapses sideways, and Bergeron lifts his sword as he moves toward him. Suddenly, Nathaniel springs toward Bergeron and thrusts his sword deeply into Bergeron's gut. Bergeron gasps, drops his sword, and falls.

Nathaniel struggles to his feet and goes to Bergeron, placing his sword to Bergeron's throat.

"As you said, we can be permanently killed and I know how to do it, too." He looks at Bergeron's wound. "Today, however, you'll recover but know that if you make any further attempts to find Belle be assured I'm prepared to finish the job or die trying and so is she."

Nathaniel sheathes his sword and starts to limp away.

"What did she name him?" Bergeron calls out in a strained voice.

Nathaniel stops. "What makes you so sure it's a boy?"

"What did she name the child, then?"

Nathaniel turns to Bergeron. "Miranda. We call her Rani."

"Rani." Bergeron nods. "It's what I called my sister. Nice to know Belle sometimes listened to me."

His head drops as his breathing becomes shallow. Nathaniel leaves him.

The following day, as Bergeron enters his castle, he's greeted by his lead servant. "My Lord, you could not find her?"

"She's dead."

The servant considers this. "Dead, my Lord?"

Bergeron fixes his stare on the man. "Yes. Dead."

The servant straightens and points his eyes away from Bergeron. "I understand, my Lord. Will you be dining at your accustomed hour?"

"Yes, that will be fine. Otherwise, I will tolerate no disturbances."

Renee makes her way through the catacombs of the Globe Theater to the area where she collects the prompt book for the nightly performances. Bowing to the restrictions placed on theaters during Elizabeth's reign, she's dressed in men's clothing and wears a fake beard that loops over her ears and is secured around her mouth with spirit gum when she's performing. Tonight it's mainly for show, since she'll be in the prompter's box all evening.

The troop is performing Cymbeline and it's the fourth performance, so the playwright is still tweaking the script. Renee noted quite a few revisions the night prior, owing to less than stellar audience reactions to the first two stagings. Last night several scenes had been rewritten and seemed to be better received, though Charles confided to Renee that, in his view, "It's still a convoluted mess."

The script is not in the regular spot where Renee usually finds it, and the company manager is nowhere to be found. She checks the door to the room where props are stored and finds it unlocked, so she goes in. A person is seated at a makeshift desk, bent over what appears to be the manuscript, with a quill pen in one hand. Renee is surprised to find it's a woman she recognizes from court, Emilia Lanier.

Emilia, the daughter of court musician Baptista Bassano, lived in the household of Henry Carey, first cousin to the Queen (and rumored to be her half-brother), but was hastily married off to another musician, Alfonso Lanier, when she became pregnant. Renee had heard rumblings about it around the time it happened, including much speculation on who the actual father was, since it seemed unlikely the elderly Carey had been up to the challenge. One name dominated the rumors, Henry Wriothesley, the young Earl of Southampton, who had once been a resident of Cecil House, next door to the household maintained by Carey when he served as Lord Chamberlain. Emilia named the boy Henry, which did little to quell the controversy.

"Emmie? Why are you here?"

Emilia looks up and stares for several seconds at Renee. "Your voice seems familiar but not your beard."

"Yes. Sorry." Renee removes the beard. "Renee Fox. My husband, Charles, and I met you at Hampton Court during one of the Queen's birthday celebrations. I think it was just before you married Alfonse."

Emilia raises a finger. "You're not supposed to be on-stage, you know."

"I'm not. I'm prompting tonight."

"Six of one. What can I do for you, Renee?"

"I came to get the script for tonight. Where's Shaxper?"

"Probably getting drunk somewhere as is usual before a performance. Shaxper has nothing to do with the process other than the fact that I've been paying him to stand in for me at curtain calls. I strenuously regret that decision, as he's started bragging to people he's the author."

"You're writing the plays?" Renee considers this. "Well, then, this explains why the playwright is so fond of having women disguise themselves as men. I don't need to tell you you're not supposed to be doing that, either."

"It pays to have once been the adornment of the Lord Chamberlain."

"Henry knew?"

"Not officially, of course. You think he bought an entire theatre just to stage plays by Kit Marlowe, before having him eliminated?"

"Yes, I was always somewhat suspicious of that. You know, Charles has stated that he doesn't find this one quite up to your usual standards."

"It's not entirely mine. The account in Holinshed is reasonably comprehensive, but short on dramatic dialogue, so I borrowed a lot from quite a few sources. Plus, I let Middleton take a crack at some scenes when I wasn't certain where to go with them."

"Middleton. Charlie guessed Wilkins."

"Now that you know who the author is, I shouldn't need to tell you to be quiet about this, for obvious reasons."

"Oh, there's no way I'm not telling Charlie."

Emilia thinks this over.

"All right. But otherwise, please keep it between your-selves. As you say, quite a few heads could roll because of this."

"Don't worry. Without going into too many details, I can assure you we're excellent at keeping secrets." She assumes a more jovial tone. "Suddenly, a certain person mentioned in the Sonnets makes a lot more sense."

Emilia shakes her head. "Shaxper writing sonnets is more ridiculous than the plays. Still, as long as people believe he wrote them, no one has made the connection."

"So, how was he?"

"An overly anxious teenage boy. But, perhaps it led to the man he's become. I do enjoy some benefits from the association."

"I certainly hope so."

Emilia thumbs through the manuscript, checking her changes, then closes it and hands it to Renee. "All done. Happy prompting."

There's an equation every long-timer must do whenever getting involved with short-timers, called "facing the numbers."

Renee and Charles have explained: "Under the most optimistic of circumstances, a shorttimer can hope to live into his or her first century but not much further, while a long-timer can easily reach a millennium and beyond."

Katie finds herself with just such a dilemma.

Totally enamored with Francis Stone, Katie knows that the best she can hope for in a relationship is a few decades of happiness, followed by watching him inevitably slide into old age and eventually death. The simple answer, of course, would be to tell Francis about her lifespan, damn the consequences, but Katie has struggled with pursuing this course.

Tonight, they've been at the opera, watching The Magic Flute with Bethany and her date, but afterward went their separate ways and Francis insisted on seeing Katie home. Now they're having tea in her living room, discussing the topics of the day. She enjoys conversations with Francis, though sometimes they can begin to anticipate what the other will say and start to sound like her parents when they're in character onstage.

"The opera was lovely. I regard it among Mozart's best work."

"Have you seen Don Giovanni?"

"I have, but I prefer the lighter operas. More playful. I don't always go to the theater with a desire to contemplate the human condition."

"You're doing that regardless of whether you're watching comedy or tragedy. It's just that with one you're laughing and the other you're crying."

"As you well know, there's enough to cry about without being reminded on stage."

"Surely you've starred in your share of both. Which do you prefer?"

She considers this. "I don't really have a preference when it comes to performing. They both present their own special challenges. Comedy is much harder, believe me. If you're off one night the audience detects it right away. With tragedy you can always incorporate any bad feelings."

Francis leans back with his arms resting on the arms of the chair and crosses his legs, giving Katie his full attention.

"What I like is losing myself in character. Totally immersing myself in whatever situation the person is enduring. It's very compelling to be able to take that on, knowing you'll be able to leave it behind at the end." She scoots to the edge of her seat and leans toward him, holding up her hands to emphasize her points. "You know, there's a school of thought in Russian theater that says you have to connect the emotions you're playing onstage to something in your own experience. To present a true emotion, not just something made up for the stage."

"An interesting prospect. How long were you in Russia?"

Katie is caught off guard by the question and pauses while she thinks of a number more plausible than the fifteen plus years she was actually there. "A few years, off and on — I split my time between Moscow and Vienna for several years."

"Did you pick up any of the vernacular?" Without waiting for a response, he says in Russian, "Are you as convincing on stage in Russian as you are in English?"

"I'd like to think so," she replies, in Russian. "Where did you learn it?"

"Bethany and I spent some time there a few years back," he says, returning to English. "She had a job at a girls' school, and I was doing a rotation in medical school. They're ideas on medicine are as different as their ideas on theater, I grant you."

"You and Beth are quite the world travelers. I wonder why we never ran into one another."

"Who knows? It's a big world, though the railway has made it a bit more accessible. We do attend the theater wherever we are, though, so if you were performing we'd have seen you."

"You and your sister are awfully close. Do you do everything together?"

"She and I are all we have. We lost our parents at a relatively young age and we've had to look out for one another since then. It helps that we have many interests in common, so we enjoy doing things together." He slides to the edge of his chair and takes Katie's hand. "But I think she'd understand if I said I'm glad she's not here now."

Katie gives him a demur smile, and blushes. "I think she'd understand if I said I am too."

As the evening moves on, they move to the settee where Francis puts his arm around Katie. She lays her head on his shoulder.

"Why won't you tell me anything about yourself?" Francis asks.

"You're not exactly a fountain of information either. What mysterious secret are you hiding?"

Francis hesitates, as though considering something. Finally, he continues. "I'm not hiding anything. I just don't talk about myself very much."

"So I'm supposed to then?"

"Just tell me where you were born, what your parents were like. Basic information."

She considers it, then responds with the backstory

she's developed for Katerina. "My parents were enter-
tainers who traveled extensively on the continent. I never
spent much time in any one place growing up. And you?"

"My father was a landowner, but he ended up on the
wrong side in a political squabble and lost everything."

"Sounds dramatic. You seem to have done well in spite
of that."

"We're doing fine now, but there were some rough
years."

"What's your favorite memory from childhood? I imagine it includes your sister."

"To an extent. I enjoyed it whenever our family was together. We'd always sing songs, have great feasts. Everyone would be there."

"What sort of songs did you sing?"

"Can I even remember?" He hums a bit before singing a
few bars of an old Celtic song Katie recognizes.

"Traditionalists were you? I don't think I've heard Celtic in— well, for a while."

"We were proud of our heritage. I'm surprised you recognized it."

"Whenever I'm in a region, I try to immerse myself in
the local dialects. I've spent quite a bit of time in Ireland
and Scotland at an impressionable age."

Their conversation trails off. Francis touches her cheek.
She looks up at him and he moves in for a kiss.

"A girl could grow accustomed to that."

"I hope so." He kisses her again.

Hearing that Amanda has fallen ill, Roland calls at
the Baynes residence. A young man whose features bear
elements of both Johnny and Amanda's faces greets him
at the door.

"Yes sir?"

"Hello, my name is Edward Fox. My father, Roland,
knew Jonathan and Amanda and he made me promise
if I ever made it to Perth, I would stop in to pay my respects."

"Welcome Mr. Fox. I'm Jeremy. My parents mentioned

your father rather frequently, I recall. Unfortunately, Mother has been ill, and her condition has worsened in the past few days. She's at Memorial Hospital."

"I'm sorry to hear that. Is she taking visitors?"

"Yes. But Mom isn't always fully there and often has trouble remembering folks."

"Perhaps I'll stop by there next, then. Take my chances."

Roland remains at the homestead for a while, chatting about the family and other topics. Afterward, he heads to the hospital where he finds Amanda's room and discovers a teen woman with short dark hair seated next to the bed.

"Good evening, ma'am."

The young woman looks up at him then stands and goes to the doorway.

"Good evening. I'm Jane. Are you here to visit my grandmother."

"Yes. Edward Fox. My father knew your grandparents some years ago. I heard she was ill, so I thought I'd stop in." He glances toward the bed. "How's she doing?"

"She drifts in and out of consciousness. When she's up, she usually recognizes people, but not always."

Roland nods.

"Would you like to sit with her a few minutes?"

"I wouldn't want to intrude on your time with her."

"Not at all. It would give me the opportunity to freshen up and grab a bite to eat."

Roland gives her a slight bow. "I'd like nothing more than to spend a little time with her."

Jane pats his shoulder then leaves and Roland sits at Amanda's bedside. Her hair is now white, and her face wrinkled, but Roland can still see vestiges of the woman he knew. He takes her hand. "Hello again Mandy. You probably can't hear me, but I wanted to let you know I was here. I didn't think I'd be able to see you, but I'm glad I'm here."

He breaks off his talk and looks away. Amanda stirs then opens her eyes and looks up at him.

"Roland? Is that you?"

Roland turns his eyes back to her and smiles. "It's me,

Mandy. I had to come and see you when I heard you were bad off."

"You look just like I remember you. How can that be?"

"That's just the way I am, Mandy. I don't age like everybody else does. That's why—" He stops then smiles at her again. "It's why I had to leave."

"You thought you had to hide that from us? Johnny and me? We were your friends. We'd have understood."

"Maybe so, but you were just two people out of a lot of others who might not have."

Amanda looks toward the ceiling. "When Johnny died, I didn't know how to get in touch with you. I didn't even know if you were alive. I wish you could have been there."

"It's the hardest thing I've ever done. Johnny was the best friend I ever had. In a lot of ways, the two of you were closer than family to me. I'll never forgive myself for not being here for you, for Johnny."

"Don't be so hard on yourself, Roland. You did what you thought you had to do." She smiles at him. "You're here now."

"I'm here as long as you need me. You just say the word."

"That won't be much longer. The doctors try to cheer me up by saying I'll be home soon, but I know." She releases Roland's hand then pulls herself up into a sitting position and holds out her hands. He takes them. "There's something I want you to do for me."

"Anything."

"My sister. Vickie. I never knew what happened to her. Things got so hectic when we were released and came to Perth, I just stopped sending letters home. Then when I tried to send another some years later, I never got a response. I'm certain—" Her voice cracks and she pauses to collect herself. "I'm sure she's dead and gone by now, but if you could find out, that would mean so much to me."

"Sure."

"And if you find her still alive, tell her—" her voice cracks again. "Tell her I've never forgotten all she did for me when we were children in the orphanage. I'm sorry I never thanked her for that."

"I'll tell her. If I find her, I'll certainly tell her."

Amanda lowers herself back onto the bed. "Thank you."

Roland debates his next idea for several seconds then leans forward. "Mandy, there's something I need to tell you. Something I've wanted to tell you for a while now—"

She holds up her hand. "I know, Roland. I know."

He eyes her curiously. "How long have you known?"

She looks away with a sad smile on her face. "Probably since before I married Johnny. At first I wasn't sure, but then it was pretty obvious."

"Why didn't you say anything?"

"You were always such a good friend. I never imagined you as anything else."

He closes his eyes and nods.

"I'm sorry I couldn't feel the same. With Johnny, I knew he was the one. I'm sorry I couldn't feel that way about you."

"That's all right." Roland gives her a half-smile. "I'm just glad I had the opportunity to know you both."

Amanda pats his hand. Roland sits with her for a few more minutes until she drifts off into sleep. When Jane returns he reports that he exchanged a few words with Amanda, then excuses himself.

"It has been a pleasure meeting you, Jane."

"You as well, Mr. Fox."

In the hallway, a few paces from the door, he turns back. "I couldn't be there for you, Mandy, but I promise you I'll always be here for your family. However long they need me."

Eleanor exits a theater on Broadway and heads toward the closest elevated steam train. A few moments later, Francis exits behind her.

"Elle, where are you going? There's still another four acts left."

She stops and turns to him.

"Yes. And I'm not going to be here to see them."

He approaches her.

"I thought you were excited to see this."

"No. I wasn't. You wanted me to be, but I really didn't care and I'm pretty sure I made that clear to you."

"You always say that and then you always enjoy yourself. What am I supposed to think?"

"What? I wouldn't say sitting, bored out of my mind, through a play is enjoying myself. If it hasn't dawned on you, I'm not a theater goer. This extravagant social life you and Beth lead just isn't for me."

"Okay, so we won't take you to anymore theater."

"It's not just theater. I don't enjoy the clubs, the concerts, the talks. I just sit there worrying who needs me at the hospital."

"Of course. The hospital. I should have known. You overwork yourself, Elle. Beth and I take you places to help get your mind off all your responsibilities. There's nothing wrong with making time for yourself."

"I don't want time for myself. Maybe you need time away from all your concerns, but I'm not like that. I feel better when I'm working. Like I have a purpose."

"I suppose that's where you're headed now."

"Yes. I probably will."

"All right. Perhaps we just need some time to think all this over and we can talk about it when you get back."

She looks away from him then exhales forcefully. "So, Beth didn't tell you."

"Tell me what?"

She shakes her head. "I'm not going back to the townhouse. I've found an apartment closer to the hospital."

"You what? When did this happen?"

"I signed the lease Tuesday."

"Tuesday? When were you planning to tell me?"

"I told Beth. She said she'd talk to you about it."

"Well she didn't. Why didn't you just tell me yourself?"

"Oh, I don't know. Maybe because I thought you'd blow a gasket. Sort of like you're doing now."

"How would you expect me to respond, dropping this on me with no warning."

"There have been quite a few warnings, Francis, for longer than I can recall. We've just never wanted to acknowledge them."

"Such as."

"Look, I'm not going to stand here in the middle of Manhattan and hash all this out with you right now. It's been painfully obvious, to me for at least the past century, that things just haven't been working with us. Open your eyes for once."

He throws up a finger, then checks himself. "This isn't over. We're going to discuss it whether you want to or not, but unlike you, I'd like to see the rest of this show."

He turns to head back into the theater. "I'll contact you at the hospital after we've had more time to reflect on this."

"Fine. It's not going to accomplish anything but—whatever."

Francis goes back inside. Elle looks after him for a long moment then decides against taking a train, and instead walks toward downtown to clear her head, sometimes thinking out loud.

"Why did I let this go on for so long?"

She recalls meeting Francis at the clinic she ran during Elizabeth's reign. When he first came in, he seemed to suspect something was different about her. Learning he and Bethany were like her lifted a weight from her shoulders.

"Maybe that's why I got so invested. I thought I owed you. Of course, you didn't seem to want to dissuade me on that."

She is, without a doubt, certain of the cause of her discontent, however.

"As much as you and Bethany reminded me that I needed to learn to enjoy herself, I never felt comfortable doing so. Even when you sprang for an assistant to help out in the clinic, I didn't feel right leaving him in charge for so long without me. And you're always telling me the hospitals have full staffs and much support. You just never got it. They're putting their lives at risk treating the sick; I'm not."

At length, she realizes she's in the vicinity of the hospital where she's working and heads there.

"Nurse Goolsby, what brings you in?"

"Hello, Nurse Pritchett. I'm hoping there's an opening in the schedule. My evening plans fell through, so I thought I'd pop in and pick up a shift if available."

"Oddly enough, we're all full up tonight." Nurse Pritchett considers it and hold up a finger. "But there is a clinic around the corner where I sometimes fill in. They're extremely busy and short-staffed and called to see if I was available. If you're interested, I could put in a good word for you."

"That would be wonderful. Thanks."

Charles is in the sitting room of their London flat reading the paper when Katie comes in, somewhat flustered.

"Is anyone staying at our villa in Tuscany?"

He lowers the paper and looks her over. "No. Why are you asking?"

"I thought I might like to visit there for a while."

"You haven't been getting into trouble in the East End again have you?"

"No, nothing like that." He continues to give her a questioning look, so she sits beside him. "Truth be known, I've met a gentleman."

"And?"

"And nothing, I've met him, and he's very taken with me, and I'm somewhat taken with him as well."

"Why is that a problem?"

"You know perfectly well why. You and Mom were fortunate to find one another. The rest of us just have to stumble along in the dark."

"Bear in mind, it took us several hundred years. Have you told this young man about yourself?"

"I'm afraid to. As much as I'd hate to watch him grow old and die, I'd prefer that to having him laugh in my face or think I'm crazy."

"People can be very understanding if you give them a chance."

"I know. It's just difficult. On the one hand, I have a lot of fun with him, but on the other, what's supposed to happen when he's seventy and I'm still in my twenties as far as the world can tell?"

"It's just one of those things you deal with, and running away is no solution. That's what got your brother in trouble, remember?"

She rolls her eyes. "It's not like I'm defrauding anyone."

"You're defrauding yourself and this young man. Now whatever you decide to do, I'll support you. But you at least owe him an explanation."

"Perhaps I'll write him a note. Yes, that's it, I'll write him a note and post it this morning."

"That's not what I meant."

"I know, Dad, but please, just let me handle this my way."

He gives her a hug.

"I just hope you don't come to regret this".

"You and me both."

The following morning, Katie is at the docks waiting to board a ship which will take her to Amsterdam. An attendant comes by and asks, "Do you have your ticket, Miss?"

"Vos, Katrina Vos." Katie speaks with a Germanic accent. "Yes, I'm all squared away."

Roland pulls up to the Marriott and an attractive, petite woman with strawberry blonde hair and holding a rose flags him down. She gives him an address in Perth which he recognizes.

"You going to the cemetery, ma'am?"

"Yes. I'm doing some family research."

"Family, eh? Let me guess, you're researching someone who got transported, aren't you?"

"Yes. I suppose you get a lot of people like that."

"Good number. If you're interested in the immigrant experience, I can recommend a number of other locations where you can find info on relatives who were transported."

"I might just take you up on that. Thanks."

When they arrive, the woman pays Roland and asks him not to wait for her.

"Sure thing, ma'am, but remember, if you need transportation while in Australia, just call on Roland Renard, okay?"

He hands her his card.

"Certainly. Take care, Roland."

He sits for a moment and watches as she makes her way across the cemetery.

"Hello. She's headed straight for Johnny and Mandy." He chuckles. "Well, Jane'll find you if that's where you end up."

The following day Roland is back at the hotel after receiving a request from the woman from the day before. He catches sight of her heading toward his cab and opens the back door for her.

"Hope your previous excursion went well, ma'am."

"It certainly did."

She slides into the back seat. Roland gets behind the wheel.

"Where to today, ma'am?"

"Someplace away from the city with an excellent view and not too many tourists. I want you all to myself today."

Roland thinks of a few likely destinations then snaps his fingers. "I know just the place to start."

He takes her to a small park on a hillside overlooking the ocean. Exiting the cab, she gives Roland a thumbs up then asks him to join her on a bench overlooking the waterfront.

"It didn't occur to me until after you were gone yesterday, but Renard is French for Fox, isn't it?"

"That's right, ma'am, it is."

"Even if I had remembered that I'm not sure I'd have made the connection to Charles and Renee." Roland turns to face her, with a questioning look. "But you definitely have your mother's eyes."

"You know my parents?"

"They're two of my closest friends, even though I haven't seen them in a very long time."

Roland grins. "You're one of us, aren't you?"

"I am. But I'd rather talk about someone who wasn't."

"All right. Who might that be?"

She pauses and stares out at the ocean for several moments.

"I want you to tell me everything you can remember about Amanda Seely."

"Mandy? How do you know her?"

"She's my sister."

He snaps his fingers again then points. "You're Vickie!"

"That's me."

"That's why you went to the graveyard yesterday." He shakes his head. "It's funny, but I feel like I already know you to some extent, at least the way she remembered you. You're about all she ever talked about."

"A lot has changed since then."

"Indeed it has. Where should I begin?"

He spends the rest of the day telling her about all his dealings with the Baynes family and of Amanda's final request that Roland find Vickie.

"Sorry to say I never got around to that. Guess you found me instead." He faces away from her. "I loved your sister, and Johnny was probably the best friend I've ever had. I knew I couldn't end up with Mandy, so I was damned glad she and Johnny made a life together. They were a good couple and raised a wonderful family."

"Which, to this day, you watch over. Mandy would be flattered. And she'd also tell you enough! The Baynes family is doing fine on its own. She'd have never wanted you to give up your life, regardless of how much time you have, for something like this."

"I know you're right and I know Mandy and Johnny would want me to move on. But the question remains, where to move on to? It's not like I've been an expert at figuring out how to conduct my affairs."

Victoria rubs his shoulder. "I'll make a deal with you. Whenever you're ready, look me up, okay?"

Roland considers this and nods. "I like that idea. Maybe just what I need to get my life back on track." He glances at her. "You wouldn't happen to be seeing anyone right now, would you?"

"Yes and no. We're not really seeing each other, but I've been involved with this great woman for several decades.

Her health has been declining, but I'm committed to being there for her."

"I see commitment runs in both our families."

"And even if I wasn't, you have one thing I usually don't look for in a mate."

"Let me guess." He points below his belt and she nods. "What is it about these Seely sisters? They just break my heart every time."

Rani Fox sits in the jiggling coach beside her mother and glances across at her uncle, Nathaniel, who's seated in the center of the seat, using one hand to steady himself. They have been traveling for many days, first in a coach, then a boat, then another coach. The country they're in has changed, but Rani doesn't detect much difference from the countryside through which they were traveling; trees give way to open fields, then more trees, dotted with occasional people, some on horseback, others guiding pack animals, but they're usually few and far between.

They're heading to a place called Kent, where Rani has never been to see people she's never met, her grandparents, Renee and Charles, her aunt Katherine, and uncle Roland. Isabella has told Rani that her grandparents are much older than she and Nathaniel but will appear to be only slightly older. Rani is not quite sure what to expect. Other than household servants, who appear not to have inherited their attributes, she has rarely seen others. She's grown accustomed to watching the people around her age and die while she remains in what appears to be her late teens. Isabella says this is common for people like them.

"I don't feel different." Rani has raised this point with her mother and uncle frequently. "I suppose I feel normal, whatever that means."

"That's to be expected." Isabella is usually nonchalant about the situation. "We are as we are, so for us, this is normal."

What Rani doesn't consider normal is that she's rarely heard any mention of her father, aside from the acknowledgement from Isabella and Nathaniel that she has one. They both know who he is, but simply refuse to talk about him beyond a few vague references that suggest quite a bit of animosity. Rani has decided that her father is still alive, as far as anyone knows, and from the few specifics she's heard from her mother, he's a long-timer as are the rest of them. Rani has yet to even hear his name mentioned.

They hit a particularly rough patch and are jarred terribly, bouncing and swaying hard to the left and right. Nathaniel gives the pair across from him a disgusted look. "Someone should seriously consider maintaining these paths better. The Romans knew to pave theirs."

At length, the road evens out and they continue with less trouble.

So far, Rani's life has been very controlled and uneventful. Splitting the family's time between France and Saxony, the most excitement comes when it's necessary to move to prevent any of the locals from noticing they haven't aged. Since both manors are well-stocked, they rarely take many household items with them; they just hop into a coach and take off as though it's just another routine trip through the countryside leaving the servants to explain their absence. It's often many years before they return.

She's been taught by private tutors, who developed her knowledge of Greek and Latin, taught her a variety of languages Isabella deemed helpful in navigating the world, and trained her in the natural sciences.

"What should I call them?"

Isabella puts her arm around Rani. "Call them whatever you want."

"What do you call them?"

"We say 'Mother' and 'Father'," Nathaniel replies. "Perhaps 'Grandma' and 'Grandpa' for you."

"Just play it by ear." Isabella gives Rani a squeeze. "They won't mind whatever you say."

"Have you told them about me?"

"I said I had a surprise for them without going into details."

"Do you think they will like me?"

Nathaniel waves his hand before Rani. "What's not to like? You're perfectly charming."

"Yes. You needn't worry about that. They won't be disappointed."

"Despite who my father is."

Isabella looks away from Rani. "That won't matter. Once they meet you, they'll accept you for who you are, not who he is."

"I wish you'd tell me more about him."

"I've told you all you need to know. He's a very bad man and you're best removed from him. I shudder to think what might happen if he knew where we were."

"Is this why we are going to England?"

"No. We need a change of scenery. Plus it's been a while since we've seen our parents or siblings, so we thought it was time for a reunion."

Nathaniel shifts in his seat. "Actually, we've never met our siblings."

"True, plus there are several hundred years separating us."

Rani takes all this in. "Good to know I'm not the only one who'll be in the dark on some introductions."

"We'll be making up a lot as we go, definitely," Nathaniel says.

When they arrive at the manor, Rani identifies four people waiting outside the main entrance, two men and two women. She assumes the older ones are her grandparents.

Once they've stopped and the coachman opens the door to let them out, Isabella presents Rani to the older couple. "Mother and Father, this is Rani, my daughter."

"Your daughter." Renee gives Charles a surprised look. "Is she—"

Isabella nods. "She's been around since the middle of the last century."

First Renee, then Charles hugs Rani, and Renee tells her, "You are most welcome here, you dear girl."

Rani turns to the younger people she assumes are Katherine and Roland. "You are my aunt and my uncle."

Katherine takes a sideways glance at Roland. "That's right."

"And yet, I am older than you."

They laugh and Roland points at her. "Not by much."

Katherine links her arm in Rani's and guides her away from the older people.

"This is special, meeting both our siblings and a niece we didn't know we had. A nice surprise indeed."

"Yes. I am happy to be with others near me in age."

"I'll bet you are," Roland says. "You'll have to fill us in on how it is living on the continent. Neither of us has made it there — yet."

While Rani is engaged with Roland and Katie, Renee speaks confidentially to Isabella. "Do you know—"

Isabella holds up her hand. "Yes." She faces Charles. "It's someone you know." She pauses. "Someone named Bergeron."

"Bergeron."

"Yes. And we have a lot to fill you in on the topic," Nathaniel adds. "He seems to have changed quite a bit from when you first informed us of him. Not for the better."

Charles considers it for a moment then he kisses Isabella's cheek. "No matter. I can see Rani has a good heart, and I know her mother and uncle have done a great job raising her."

Renee concurs. "Yes. I'm looking forward to getting to know her and catching up with you both. It's so nice to finally have the whole family together under the same roof, especially with such a wonderful surprise."

"Don't expect that any of you are getting away for a few years." Charles extends his hand inviting them inside. "We're long overdue for a reunion and plan to take all the time in the world to enjoy it."

Still Crazy After
All These Years

Once their run in a variety show at the Empire Theater in New York is done, Charles and Renee spend several months touring the South and Midwest as Carlton and Carlotta. At last, Renee grows tired of all the touring and performing and announces she's taking a break. Charles has been offered a role in an off-Broadway showcase back in New York and decides to take it. He bids Renee farewell as she takes off for New Zealand with an eye toward taking an extended vacation there and visiting Roland in Australia.

One evening as Charles is preparing to leave the theater, he's met by two police detectives, Ware and Cranston.

"Do you know a man named William Openshaw?" Ware says.

"Openshaw. Why do I know that name?" Charles considers it then snaps his fingers. "Yes, Willie. I know him."

"When was the last time you saw him?" Cranston says.

"Not for a month or more. I used to rent a room at his row house in Brooklyn. Is he missing?"

"Not exactly," Ware says. "Can you account for your whereabouts Tuesday between nine and eleven p.m.?"

"I was here. The evening performance ends around ten-thirty to ten forty-five and I'm on stage until the end. I usually spend fifteen or twenty minutes changing and getting out of my makeup. After a performance cast members will usually get together at a pub down the road, but that night I just headed home which would have been around eleven-fifteen to eleven-thirty." He shoots his eyes back and forth between the detectives. "Has something happened to Willie?"

"He was shot to death two nights ago," Cranston says. "Outside his row house in Brooklyn."

Charles shakes his head. "That's awful. I can't imagine who'd want to hurt him. He could be a bit of a stickler for the rent, but otherwise a pleasant fellow."

"Would you mind coming down to the station with us to answer some questions?" Ware says.

"Certainly, if you think it would help."

At the station, Charles has his fingerprints taken.

"To rule you out since you were in the house," Ware tells him.

Afterward, Charles is seated at a desk with the two detectives.

"What can you tell us about your time rooming at Mr. Openshaw's place?" Cranston says.

"Not a lot. I'd see him coming and going. Sometimes he'd be away for several days. I think there was another renter, a guy named Melvin or Nelvin, but I don't know much about him and couldn't even tell you if that was his first or last name."

"How'd you meet Mr. Openshaw?" Ware says.

"Mutual acquaintances. My wife left New York several months ago but I had already gotten a role in the play I'm doing, so I inquired around about places I could stay. One of my cast mates told me about the room at Willie's. We met, shook hands and I moved in a few days later."

"Why'd you leave?" Ware says.

"It was a temporary arrangement from the start. I prefer having a place all to myself when my wife's not around. When the play's run was extended, I found my current flat in the Village and moved a few weeks after moving in."

"Would you have any idea why anyone would want to kill him?" Cranston says. "Was he seeing anyone that you know of?"

Charles shakes his head. "Not that I recall. Mind you, the person who referred me to him suggested he was quite the ladies' man, but I never saw it. If he was seeing anyone they must have been meeting at her place."

"You said there was a third person living there," Ware says. "What can you tell me about him?"

"Not very much. I can't swear he was even living there. I know there was an extra room and every now and then I'd see another man either entering or leaving. He always had a hat and coat on, so I never got a good look at him. One morning I heard someone in the hallway and Willie called out 'See you Melvin' or 'Nelvin'."

"Did you ever ask Openshaw about him?" Cranston says.

"Wasn't any of my business. I just assumed he was staying there and kept to himself."

Ware looks over the notes he's been taking, then leans in to confer with Cranston.

"Will you be staying in town, Mr. Fox?" Cranston asks.

"The play closes in a few days and I'd planned to return to England, but I haven't made any arrangements yet and if need be, I can stick around."

"If you don't mind," Cranston says. "How can we reach you if we have more questions?"

Charles takes out a card. "This is my solicitor, that is, the attorney who handles my business affairs in New York. If all else fails, he'll know how to reach me." On back, he writes the address of his flat and the phone number at the theater. "The stage manager at the theater should also know how to get a message to me if the play has closed."

The detectives release Charles. Two weeks later, Ware lets the attorney know Charles is no longer needed for the case, and he makes plans to leave for England.

Bethany Tremaine and her brother Francis are at the apartment they own just a few blocks from Syracuse University. Francis is finishing up his latest medical degree and is interning at a nearby hospital. Since the beginning of the 20th century, he has rarely practiced medicine outside of a hospital, preferring the research aspects to actual hands-on care-giving, but he enjoys the interactive nature of the internship and the opportunity to brush up on current medical practices. Bethany is studying music with a special interest in Celtic music and songs, which they used to sing around their family's home many centuries before.

One of their methods for hiding in plain sight is to conceal their identities and misreport their relationship with one another. While they've been living in this area, Bethany has been using the surname Stone and Francis introduces himself as Bethany's cousin Frank.

Today they're discussing Bethany's recent love life,

with one man being the focus of their talk.

"Might I remind you, dear sister, that you know very little about this Enzo Morelli."

"I know how I feel. Enzo's goofy but in a very endearing way. Besides, who is it who's always saying, 'Follow your heart'?"

"Follow your heart but don't ignore your head. Since it's almost a foregone conclusion that he's a short-timer you could be opening yourself up to all sorts of problems."

"He might be he might not be. It's not like there's a test for it."

"Well." Francis thinks better of it. "Never mind."

Bethany looks at him through narrowed eyes. "You weren't going to propose that test we heard about from that horrible man we met in Rome were you? What was his name — Bergeron?"

"Well, it would settle things, but then again, if he's not one of us, it wouldn't be good at all. My stitching skills still aren't what they should be given how many times I've been through the ER rotation."

Bethany stands and goes to the window. She looks out for several seconds then turns back to Francis. "Why all the concern anyway? I've dated numerous men throughout my life. You never got much up in arms about them."

"I don't think you appreciate how taken this young man is with you. I took the opportunity to observe the two of you when you were at the diner the other night and he's smitten. I wouldn't be surprised if he produced a ring at your next encounter."

"That's silly." Then she takes on a curious expression. "At least I seriously doubt he'd do something like that."

"What if he does, though. Are you prepared to live with the consequences of getting involved that deeply with someone who'll only be around a fraction of your life?"

She doesn't respond.

"Caught you with that one, didn't I?"

"Maybe a little."

"And let's not forget children. How would you handle them, especially if they're not like us?"

"If it happens, I'll deal with it then." She walks toward

him with her arms crossed. "Honestly, with your romantic history, you're hardly one to lecture me on my love life."

"Ah yes, Elle. I've never met someone with whom I've had so much in common yet been so incompatible. You'd think after sniping at one another for nearly three hundred years, I'd have realized how toxic our relationship was."

"Yes, that is true, but she's not who I meant."

"Then who are you talking about?"

"You know that actress, Kat—, Kath—"

"Katerina Fuchs. See, I was in the same boat with Kate that you're in now. I know whereof I speak."

"You should have at least told her about your lifespan."

"Have you told Enzo about yours?"

"No. Not yet."

"What are you waiting for, him to turn eighty with you still looking as young and lovely as you do now?"

"No. Probably before then."

They look at one another and break down into laughter.

"It's not exactly the same, though. With Kate I also sensed reluctance on her part. I suspected there was something she wasn't telling me about herself. Maybe she was already married."

"I never got that from her, but she did disappear awfully fast given how much time we'd spent together up until that point. Nothing happened between you did it?"

"Like what?"

"Like anything. An argument, a misunderstanding?"

"Not that I recall. Well, I did kiss her."

"You kissed her?" Bethany perks up.

"Yes, a couple of times. She seemed to enjoy it — certainly didn't try to stop me. Next day, she was gone. All I got was this cryptic note stating, 'It simply won't work between us.'"

"That's really strange."

"Kate was hard to understand at times. She was very intelligent and obviously well educated, but she wouldn't talk about any of that. I could hardly get her to talk about the simplest things like when she was born or what became of her parents."

"How often did you tell her those things about yourself? I can't imagine you confiding in her that you were born under Henry V and had to leave England because our father sided with the wrong heir to the throne."

"It didn't really come up. She didn't ask about me or talk about herself. It was all here and now for her. She was a complete enigma."

There's a knock at the door.

"Are you expecting anyone?"

"No." Bethany walks to the door. "Who is it?"

"Enzo," the person on the other side says.

Bethany glances at her brother then opens the door. Enzo Morelli is standing there. He's a tall gangly man with a thin mustache and a day's growth of beard and dark curly hair that's a little too long. His head is bouncing slightly as if in time with some music only he can hear and he keeps shifting his weight from one foot to the next making it seem like he's trying to dance.

"Hey Beth! Thought I'd surprise you."

"You sure did. Come on in."

Enzo enters but hesitates when he sees Francis. "Oh, you've got company."

"Ah, yes. This is—"

"Frank Tremaine." Francis approaches Enzo with one hand extended. "Bethany's cousin."

Bethany rolls her eyes at Francis. "Yes, my cousin Frank."

"Good to meet you Frank."

Francis shakes his hand. "I take it you're a student here as well."

"Yes. I'm studying accounting."

"Accounting," Francis says. "My guess is you'll always be employed then. Whenever my accountant starts rattling off numbers to me, it's like he's speaking a foreign language."

Enzo shrugs. "It's not that hard, but you've got to be very careful. What do you do?"

Bethany steps beside Enzo and puts her arm around

him. "Frank's a doctor, an intern, at County Medical."

"I guess you'll never be out of a job either," Enzo says with a slight grin. "People are always getting sick."

"That they are," Francis says.

Enzo looks around at the apartment. "Wow, this is a great place. I see why you wouldn't want to live on campus with a place like this."

"It's Frank's place, but he's letting me rent a room from him. Speaking of which, how exactly did you find me? I'm not listed in the directory."

"That's cool of him," Enzo says. "No, I remember you saying you lived near Bergdorf's Deli. I hung around there until I saw you and watched which building you went in." Grinning sheepishly, he concludes, "Actually yours was about the third or fourth door I knocked on. The last guy knew you and pointed me in this direction."

"Quite a bit of initiative there," Francis says.

"Yes," Bethany says. "You could have just asked where I live."

Enzo points at her. "But it wouldn't have been a surprise."

Bethany and Francis look at one another and shrug.

"You're absolutely right," she says.

"Say, you hungry?" Enzo says. "Maybe we could go out for dinner somewhere."

Bethany steps away from him. "Frank and I had plans—"

Francis interrupts. "But you're more than welcome to join us."

Bethany gives him an inquisitive look.

Enzo says, "Really? I wouldn't want to crash."

"Not a problem. It would give us the chance to get acquainted. Bethany's always so focused on her studies. I'd be interested in meeting the young man who can tear her away from all that."

The Foxes are at their loft, Charles reading The Village Voice, and Renee doing Yoga in the living area.

"Renee, listen to this. A young woman was murdered

a few nights ago."

"That's terrible."

"But listen to this part. It says her throat was cut."

Renee stops her exercises and looks at Charles.

"Where was she killed?"

"Central Park. She was jogging around seven and someone pulled her into the woods and killed her and left her body where it would be easily found. It says there have been several other murders like it in the area."

"That sounds uncomfortably like Bergeron. You don't think he's in town do you?"

"I hope not. If he is, no one's safe. Victoria especially."

"Does it give any more details?"

"No, just her age and physical description. I'll wager you she was strangled. That'd be a sure sign he was in town."

"What should we do about it?"

Charles shrugs. "I could go to the police."

"Do you think that would do any good? I mean, if you tell them what you know, you'll have to tell them how you know it and you know how they'll react."

"I know. But if it's him we can't just sit by and let that maniac get away with this."

"You're right. Wait. Who wrote the article?"

Charles checks the byline. "Rebecca J. Asher. She's listed as a staff writer."

"Might be better to see her first. She probably has more background on the killings."

"Good idea. Once I know more of the story, then I can go to the police."

"Charlie, they'll haul you off to the loony bin. But if the alternative is letting another woman get killed, then I say let's go for it. We can probably offer enough proof to bolster our claim. For one, we can send them to the Met."

Charles nods. "I'll ring her up, maybe go by the paper this afternoon. If there's time, I'll swing by the main precinct. Just be prepared to pick me up from Bellevue after that."

"If that happens, we'll deal with it."

Charles resumes reading the paper while Renee goes

back to her exercises.

Rebecca Asher sits at the desk she shares with several other reporters in the Cooper Square office of The Village Voice, reviewing a police report on the latest victim of a heinous killer, known for cutting the throats of the women he murders. She's worked as a staff reporter at The Voice since graduating from Columbia University in 2004 and most of her reporting has been about the murders. Before that, she held a variety of part-time jobs with the paper, starting the summer after arriving in NYC for her freshman year, from being a receptionist, gofer, proofreader, editorial assistant, and copywriter in the ads department. She's also one of four writers who share authorship of an occasional column entitled The Frantic Feminist.

She came to New York after graduating from Decatur High School, near her hometown of Atlanta, in 1999 to study Journalism. There, she became part of a clique of highly progressive lesbians who staged shows, sponsored talks, and agitated for change, on campus and around town. Rebecca's writing skills proved invaluable to the group and made her an important voice in the movement. For the first time in her life, she felt free, and unencumbered by the expectations of her friends and family back home and came to believe she could truly make a difference.

One evening, halfway through her junior year, as she returned to her dorm, she was startled by a familiar voice calling her name as she moved through the lobby. She turned to see a tall, middle-aged, well-tanned man with dark, curly hair approaching her. Though it had been years, she immediately recognized her father, Owen Asher.

"Owen the pilot." She used her mother's derogatory term for Owen. "What the hell are you doing here?"

"Hello, Little Bit."

Rebecca shook her head furiously. "No. Don't you call me that. Don't you ever call me that again. You gave up your right to call me that when I was nine."

"Becky, I'm sorry."

"Sorry? You ran out on us, left us to fend for ourselves while you're off being a swinging single in Tacoma, and all you can manage is sorry? Oh, by the way, Mom's dead. Don't know if you'd heard."

"I guess I deserve that."

"You guess?"

"Becky, please, I just want to try to make amends."

"No. No. Unacceptable. You think you can ditch out on your responsibilities then just waltz back in and resume playing Daddy?" She stormed away from him, then swung back. "To hell with you, Owen! Just hop back in your damn plane and fly the hell out of here."

The confrontation had drawn a crowd. Marcy, the dorm manager appeared. "Is everything okay?"

Rebecca hurried to her. "No." She pointed to Owen. "This man's stalking me. Call the cops."

"Becky, you don't have to do this." He addressed Marcy. "I'm her father."

"Noncustodial. You can verify that with the district attorney in DeKalb County, Georgia. There's a restraining order against him there, taken out by Rachel Lawson, my aunt. She's my legal guardian until I finish college."

"Sir, you're going to need to leave." Marcy assumed a protective posture between Rebecca and Owen. Over her shoulder she said to the desk attendant, "Call NYPD."

Owen threw up his hands. "That won't be necessary. I'm sorry I bothered you, Rebecca. I hope we can talk some other time."

With that, he left.

Marcy turned to Rebecca. "Are you okay?"

"Yeah. Yes. I'm great."

"You're sure. We can call the police and have them take a statement."

Rebecca threw up her hands. "No. I'm good. I just need to get to my room. I'll be fine."

She hurried to the elevator and punched the button repeatedly, with her body turned so she could still see the entrance. When the doors finally opened, she headed up to her room, shaking violently, her heart pounding. After spending nearly twenty minutes pacing around the room punching her left palm with her right hand, she retrieved a bottle of wine she and her roommate had stashed away and set it on the kitchen counter.

"Where is it?" She jerked open drawers in the kitchen, looking for the corkscrew. Instead, when she opened the drawer where they'd been filing the phone books and manuals for their appliances, the words "Are You Distressed?" popped out at her.

Rebecca stared at the words for a long moment, then removed the yellow pages with a large ad on the front for Caring Hands, Loving Hearts, a local charity.

"If you feel you're at the end of your rope, don't give up, let's talk." She glanced at the bottle of wine on the counter then nodded emphatically and retrieved her phone.

A woman with the hint of a British accent answered. "Caring Hands, this is Vickie. Who do I have the pleasure of speaking to?"

"I'm Rebecca. Becky, actually."

"Thanks for calling, Becky. Let's talk."

Before she realized it, Rebecca was pouring out her heart to this total stranger on the phone, detailing her father's abandonment when Rebecca was nine, her mother's death when Rebecca was sixteen, finally leading to her confrontation with Owen the Pilot downstairs that evening.

"That's a lot to be dealing with, Becky. But you're absolutely right that drowning yourself in a bottle of wine is not the answer. Trust me, I've been there before."

They talked for over two hours and in the end, Rebecca learned that the person on the other end of the line wasn't a total stranger, but was none other than Victoria Wells, founder of Caring Hands, Loving Hearts. It was the first of several encounters Rebecca would have with her, and they eventually became friends.

Rebecca's reading is interrupted by a voice nearby. "Ms. Asher?"

She looks to see a man with brown hair, above shoulder length, approaching her desk.

"I'm Rebecca Asher." She stands as he reaches her desk. "You must be Charles Fox."

"I am. As I mentioned on the phone, I was hoping I could talk to you about some articles you've written for the Voice, about a series of murders in New York."

"Ah, yes. Please have a seat. I was just looking over the latest police report. Nasty business."

"I wish I could say it's the first time I've seen something like this but it has the signature of someone I've known for a very long time."

"A very long time?" Rebecca leans forward and props her arms on the desk. She speaks in a low voice. "You wouldn't happen to know Victoria Wells, would you?"

Charles glances left, then right. "I certainly do. And I suspect the answer to your next question is yes."

Rebecca's eyes narrow. "So, the obvious follow up is how long have you been around?"

"Give or take a few decades, sixteen hundred ninety-five years. "

Rebecca falls back in her chair. "Wow. I mean. Wow. That's like, what? The Roman Empire?"

"Waning days."

"Does this mean you think the killer could be?"

"It seems probable. I noted in your article that the killer cuts the throats of his victims but it's probably not how he's killing them. Would you happen to know the actual cause of death?"

"It's withheld in the police reports released to the press, but I might have a contact who may have let it slip."

Charles takes this in. "Would it be strangulation?"

Rebecca reaches for her recorder. "I'm definitely going to need this."

Francis Tremaine tosses his keys onto the console table just inside the door of his apartment in Jersey City. He is coming off a 36-hour rotation at the local hospital and he's ready for a long rest. He's been living here, as Frank Tremaine, ever since Bethany called to say she missed him. They'd been separated since Bethany's marriage, which Francis attended as her cousin. The separation was Bethany's idea too, since she has not yet told her husband Enzo about her special attribute, and feels it will be easier to keep it quiet if there aren't two of them around who didn't seem to age.

Entering his bedroom, Francis' eye is drawn by the blinking light on his Phonemate answering machine. He'd purchased it and hooked it up to a secondary line which he'd set up so Bethany could reach him in case of an emergency. He's given her cards with the family name on it to give to Enzo and his father in case anything happened to her, so Francis can be there in a hurry, since it's doubtful her average lifespan family would know how to handle someone like her.

Francis pushes the play button. There's a pause, before a voice he doesn't recognize comes on. "Hello? Ah, this is Gino Morelli. I'm, ah, Bethany's father-in-law. She and Enzo — ah — there was a car accident, and they didn't make it. The children are okay."

Gino gives his phone number and Francis jots it down then picks up the phone and quickly dials.

"Mr. Morelli. This is Mr. Tremaine. You said there was an accident?"

"Oh. Yeah. Head-on collision in Jersey. I'm sorry to be the one—"

"Where is Bethany?"

"Bethany didn't make it. She was in the front of the car."

"Yes, I understand that, but I need to know where they've taken her."

"I guess to the hospital or the morgue. That's what the trooper I spoke to said."

"Do you have this trooper's name and number?"

"I can get it for you."

"Please do."

There's a few seconds of silence on the line. "Okay. It's Officer Stanley Kehoe and here's his number."

Francis writes down the information. "Thank you, Mr. Morelli."

"Hey, listen. I'm sorry about Bethany. She was a great

lady."

"Thank you. I am deeply sorry for your loss as well."

Francis hangs up and runs his hands over his eyes.

"Focus!"

He picks up the phone and dials another number.

"Hello, I'm trying to reach Officer Kehoe."

"I'll see if he's available. Please hold."

Several minutes elapse.

"Kehoe."

"Hello, Officer Kehoe. My name is Francis Tremaine. I'm told you were the responding officer at a car accident tonight which involved my sister."

"Do you mean the one on Highway 17?"

"Yes, that's the one. Do you know where they've taken the bodies?"

"The coroner retrieved them from the scene, I believe. It was just above Newark, so I assume that's where they went."

"How long ago was that?"

"Probably four and a half to five hours."

"Thank you."

Francis hangs up and dials another number in Jersey. This one takes a few minutes to connect. A gruff-sounding man answers.

"Judge Hawkins? This is Francis Tremaine."

"Francis? Do you know what time it is? Everyone's asleep."

"Yes, I'm aware of the time and I apologize, but I need an extremely important favor."

"One that won't wait until morning?"

"No, sir. My sister was involved in a car accident tonight and didn't make it."

"I'm sorry to hear that, Francis. I didn't know her, but from the way you've described her, she sounds like a wonderful lady."

"Yes. Thank you, sir, that's very kind of you to say. I'm calling to see if you could issue an injunction to have the coroner turn her body over to me right away."

"That's a rather strange request at this time of the morning. May I ask why you need this?"

"Well, sir, our family's religion has some rather strict requirements on how a body should be handled and I need to get to her in case they're planning to do an autopsy."

"I see. Then time is of the essence. I'll get to it right away."

"Thank you very much, sir and again I apologize for the late call."

"Under the circumstances, I understand. I assume you'll be heading here?"

"Yes, sir. I'll be over shortly. Oh, and could you clear things with the district attorney, so there are no problems at the coroner's office?"

"I certainly can. See you when you get here."

Francis pauses for several seconds to collect himself then dials a colleague.

"Greg? It's Francis."

"Heck of a time to be calling."

"Yeah, I know, but this is extremely important. You know how we've been talking about my abilities?"

"I do."

"How would you like an opportunity to examine one of us up close?"

"Who are we talking about?"

"My sister. If you'll give me access to your lab, I can explain it all then."

"No one's using it. You know where the keys are."

"Great, I'll meet you there."

He makes one final call to an ambulance driver he knows, then grabs his coat and heads out the door.

"Hang on, Beth, I'm coming for you."

After Charles speaks to Rebecca for nearly an hour, she accompanies him to the police station.

"They'll probably be less likely to lock you up if I'm there."

"Do you know the detective in charge?"

"Somewhat. Of course, it's possible they'll lock us both up. Who knows?"

They introduce themselves at the front desk and a few moments later, Detective Tom Rosen appears.

"Ms. Asher. Here for another 'no comment.'"

"On the contrary. I thought I'd bring you someone who might help you solve the case."

She presents Charles. "Yes, Detective Rosen, I think I can provide you with relevant information."

"Okay." Rosen spreads his hands before him then placing them on his hips. "Such as?"

"I read in the paper that all the victims had their throats cut. But Ms. Asher informs me the actual cause was withheld. I'm betting it was strangulation, am I correct?"

Rosen's eyes narrow and he points at the pair.

"That definitely earns you a trip to my desk."

Rebecca and Charles follow Rosen into the precinct. Once their seated at the desk, Rosen continues. "The detail about cause of death was withheld for a reason. I'll be interested to hear how you deduced it."

Charles gives Rebecca a raised eyebrow then turns to Rosen. "If I tell you what I know, I'll have to tell you how I know it and you won't believe me."

"Try me."

"All right. The place I've seen this before was London, the Whitechapel district, 1888."

"Hold on, hold on. You're talking about Jack the Ripper. You expect me to believe that Jack the Ripper is alive and well and living in the tri-state area? Or that you were alive then?"

"The person who did the actual Ripper killings is almost certainly long dead, but there was a copycat who used the killings to escape notice, and he is still around."

Rosen points to Rebecca. "And you believe him?"

"I do. But I have other reasons that I can't go into just now."

Charles retrieves a notepad from the desk.

"As I said, you won't believe me. However, I can provide you with enough proof that me and my wife have been around at least that long, and, by extension, the killer."

"By all means. Please do."

Charles begins jotting information on the pad.

"You'll also need my photo and fingerprints."

"If you're not the killer, why do we need your photo and prints?"

"The fingerprints, you already have. At least, I guess you still do. I was fingerprinted for a murder case some decades ago. The photo is so you can compare it to historical shots to demonstrate I'm telling the truth."

"You're serious about this. Okay. We might still have prints from that period on microfilm."

"Good." Charles writes several more lines, then slides the notepad across the desk to Rosen. "The names and dates on that sheet should lead you to enough information to support at least part of what I've told you about myself. My wife, Renee and I have been performers for a very long time. We've had publicity photos and head shots taken, news articles written about us, and we've been in movies during the silent era and early talkies. I've listed most of the names we've worked under throughout the years. I'll leave it to you to dig up the information from whatever sources you choose, so you'll know I haven't fabricated any of those."

Rosen picks up the notepad, and looks over what's written:

Charles and Renee Fox (Real names)
Charlton and Carlotta Fox 1890-1930 (England and America)
Charles and Carolina Renard 1830-1860 (France, England, and America)
Carl Renard 1810-1830 (mostly France)
Publicity photos for American tour 1895
Publicity photos for Empire theatre 1929-32
William Openshaw murder 1933 (Fingerprints)

One item catches Rosen's eye. "You worked at the Empire Theater?"

"Yes. We did a run there in the '30s, before I met Openshaw."

"Did you know someone named Dennis Wiley?"

"Wiley?" Charles thinks about it, then snaps his fingers

and points. "There was a stagehand there called Denny. I don't think I knew his last name. He was just a kid, working for tips, I believe. Why? Do you know him?"

"Maybe." Rosen dials an extension. "Janie. It's Rosen."

"Hello, Detective. What can I do for you?"

"Does your uncle still work at Lincoln Center?"

"He does."

"What does he do there?"

"He's a researcher and archivist."

"Send me his contact info. It's for a case."

Rebecca waits at the desk while Rosen leads Fox over to where mug shots are taken. He gives a front and side view. Then he's fingerprinted.

As he's wiping the ink off his fingers, Charles says, "The case I was fingerprinted for in 1933 relating to William Openshaw was never solved, I believe. It happened after my time at Openshaw's, but I rented a room from him for a few weeks and police questioned me and took my prints to rule out any false leads."

Rosen nods. "We'll see what we have."

Rosen leads Charles back to the desk where Rebecca rises and joins him.

Charles tells him, "Approach this with an open mind, detective. There are more things in heaven and on earth than can be imagined in your philosophy."

"Sounds like it."

Charles hands Rosen a card with his name and contact information on it. "Once you've confirmed my credentials, here's where you can find me and Renee."

As they're walking out, Charles says to Rebecca, "Thanks for all your help, Ms. Asher. I will definitely keep you in the loop."

Rebecca points. "You better."

Dennis Wiley sits on one of the park benches under the shade trees outside the front entrance of the senior community where he has spent the past ten years. He is nearly 90 years old yet remains as alert and spry as a man much younger. He's quick with a joke, or a story of his days in Vaudeville, or his stint in the military during WWII. Never married, he's been a "jack of all trades" and he has a story to tell about each one, making him a particular favorite among the other residents.

As he's trying to recall a snippet of a song from his childhood, he spies a familiar car pulling into a parking space. A few minutes later, his grandnephew, Tom Rosen approaches, carrying an envelope.

"Tommy, good to see you."

"How you doing, Uncle Denny?" Dennis rises to shake Tom's hand.

"Can't complain. How's your mother getting along?"

"She's doing all right. The whole family is well. She says she wants to see you at Thanksgiving dinner this year."

"Me pass up your mom's cooking? Never!"

They sit on the bench.

"You used to work at the Empire Theater, right, Uncle Denny?"

"I sure did. Back in the heyday of Vaudeville. 'Course, I didn't really work there, but they let me hang around and run errands for tips. Even gave me the title of stagehand." He looks toward the sky shaking his head. "Those were good times!"

"When you were there, did you ever run across a married couple named Charles and Renee Fox?"

Mention of the names causes Dennis's face to light up. "Charlie and Renee? Sure I knew 'em — great people and very good tippers. As I recall they performed under the names Carlton and Carlotta. One of those husband and wife acts like Burns and Allen, a little soft shoe, some songs, a few jokes. What made them stand out was that they sort of took turns playing the straight man, kept the audience off balance. Really funny, though."

"So you liked them?"

"Liked 'em? Heck, I loved 'em. At the time I thought Renee was the prettiest lady I'd ever laid eyes on and definitely one of the sweetest. And Charlie was never too busy to horse around with me and the other kids who worked around the theater."

Rosen removes the photo of Fox from the envelope and

hands it to Dennis. "Does this guy look familiar to you?"

Dennis adjusts his glasses and looks over the photo then chuckles.

"I'll be darned. If I didn't know better, I'd swear that was Charlie Fox. At least the way I remember him. But it couldn't be. They were a lot older than me back then. If they're still around they'd be pushing a hundred and twenty or more." He laughs at the thought. "So is this guy related to Charlie?"

"Haven't actually figured that out yet."

Dennis puts his finger against his chin, trying to recall something. "You know, seeing that photo made me remember something. Charlie gave me a present one time. It was a coin with some Roman guy's face on it. He said if I was ever hard up for cash, I might be able to sell it for quite a bit of dough."

"Do you still have it?"

"I sure do. It's in my room, come on."

Before Rosen can stop him, Dennis is on his feet and walking briskly back toward the entrance of the facility. Rosen hurries after him. In his room, Dennis goes to his closet and removes a lock box.

"My valuables." Dennis speaks with raised eyebrows then winks. He takes out a small envelope and dumps the contents into his hand. "There you go."

He hands Rosen a coin, dark gray green in color with the details still clear. On one side is the picture of a Roman emperor with the words "IMP CONSTANTINVS P F AVG" and on the other is a depiction probably of a god with the words "SOLI INVICTO COMITI."

"Pretty snazzy, eh," Dennis says.

"Yeah, and if it's real, pretty valuable. Have you ever had this authenticated?"

Dennis waves his hand toward Rosen. "I let a jeweler friend of mine look at it once — offered me five hundred clams on the spot for it. But I wasn't looking to sell it. It's a keepsake, you know — from a friend."

Rosen hands the coin back. "Thanks, Uncle Denny, you've been a big help."

When Gregory Norton arrives at his lab at the university hospital, the first sight he's confronted with is the badly mangled body of a woman who appears to have been in her twenties. His colleague, Francis Tremaine, is already there, wearing scrubs and preparing to make an incision.

"Good god, Francis, what is this? I thought you said I'd have this opportunity to observe someone like you."

"You will. This is my sister, Bethany. She's just a few years younger than I am."

"Yes, and apparently dead. I don't need a medical degree to see that."

"I told you, we have an incredible capacity for healing, but she's a bit more banged up than most, so we may need to assist her a bit."

"Assist? Francis, this is crazy. How long has she been like this?"

"I'm told the accident happened seven or eight hours ago."

"Rigor will have set in by now."

"It hasn't." Francis gently lifts her arm. "Feel her skin."

Greg touches her shoulder. "Still warm. That shouldn't be if she's been dead that long."

"She hasn't give up. Anymore doubts, check her liver temp."

"No. That's not necessary. What do I need to do?"

"Concentrate on any organ damage and I'll start setting the bones. Her body is no doubt already trying to repair itself; we need to deal with the worst of the damage, otherwise it might become permanent."

"Has anything like this been attempted for someone like you?"

"Not by me, but I have this theory. Whenever one of us is seriously injured, our bodies go into a type of stasis."

"You mean suspended animation?"

"Close, but not exactly. Our metabolic processes continue but slow to such an extent it seems like we're dead. It varies, however, the same as healing functions vary for regular people, which is why I needed to get Beth here as quickly as I could"

"I just hope you're right."

They work for several hours, during which Greg continues to look for signs that a normal dead body would exhibit and continues to find none. Francis points. "Greg. Look."

Greg is amazed to see the cuts on Bethany's face starting to heal.

"Incredible."

Bethany's body starts to tremble then she takes in a gasp of air and opens her eyes. It becomes apparent that she's in a lot of pain.

"I'll start a morphine drip." Greg hurries to his medical cabinet.

Bethany starts speaking, weakly, in a language Greg can't understand. Francis runs his hand over her head and softly speaks to her in the same language.

"What language is that?" Greg places a bag of saline solution onto a pole.

"It's Celtic, the first language we ever spoke. We spoke it around the house when we were kids."

"What's she saying?"

"She wants to know who we are and why she's here."

Tom Rosen is at his desk when he's notified that he has a visitor. He goes to the front desk to find a frail man with thinning brown hair, and glasses with black plastic frames. The visitor is carrying a large leather case in one hand and several books under his other arm.

"Doctor Mabry. I'm Tom Rosen. Glad you could come in today."

Mabry perks up. "Thank you, detective."

"I reserved a conference room for us." Rosen motions toward the precinct room. "Some others will be joining us."

As they walk Dr. Mabry tells Rosen: "I must say, I was intrigued by your inquiry and wonder what motivated it. It's not often I get requests from the police to research obscure 19th and 20th century personalities."

"It's unusual in my line of work to request such information, as you might imagine. But it may be relevant to a case."

"I'm pleased to report that I've found the information you requested plus some other information you'll find very interesting."

Once they're settled into the conference room, Mabry unpacks his satchel and opens one of the books he's brought. "I found a couple of books which reference stage actors from the eighteenth and nineteenth centuries and they're illustrated. I also have a volume on Vaudeville performers from the early twentieth century which references the individuals you requested, and I have a couple of videos of old films you should find very interesting. I also wanted to see how far I could trace the name, and this yielded some fascinating finds."

Mabry lays the first volume on the table, open to a bookmarked section.

"Per your instructions, I looked for performers named Fox or Renard, that being the French equivalent of Fox. This photo depicts a husband and wife act whose stage names were Carlton and Carlotta Fox. They appear to have originated in England but spent much of the early 20th century in America in various venues. I've found references to them from approximately 1905 through the early thirties when they disappear completely with no explanation for what became of them."

Rosen looks at the photo of Carlton and Carlotta and he's immediately struck by the strong resemblance of Carlton to Charles Fox.

Mabry points. "If you flip the page, there are individual photos of them." He opens a second book to a marked place and slides it over. "This is a photo of an actor named Charles Renard who was active in England and America just before the Civil War. Charles Renard appeared in plays stateside with the Booths as well as other prominent actors of the time. The next page has a photo of an actress named Katerina Fuchs, who's outside the parameters of my search, though 'Fuchs' is the German equivalent of 'Fox'. It's not stated if there's a relationship, but in my estimation, she has features in common with the

Foxes and Renards, so, she could well be an offspring."

Rosen looks over the pictures of Renard and again notes the resemblance.

Mabry continues: "I must say, when I saw these, I was certain they were from the same family, but after further examination, I think it's more than that."

"Why do you say that?"

"I'll show you." Mabry places the books together, so the pictures of Fox and Renard are beside one another. "Look here," he says pointing at a slightly noticeable scar above Renard's right eye. "And here." He indicates a similar scar above Fox's eye.

"They match."

"That's not all. Look here." He points to a jagged birthmark on Fox's left cheek near his ear then points to a similar birthmark on Renard's cheek.

"These pictures had to have been taken at least sixty years apart."

"You're right, but I'm not sure what else to conclude." He removes another book from his stack and places it on the table. "I became fascinated with these individuals, so I expanded my search and ran across mention of an actor named Claude Renard who, with his wife Renee, was active in Restoration England and in France during the same period. They were contemporaries of Moliere. It just so happens they both sat for portraits in Holland around this time."

He opens the book he set on the table to two color plates showing a portrait of a man beside that of a woman. The man looks just like Carlton and the woman like Carlotta from the later photos. "I took the extra step of contacting the British library and they confirmed that the portraits in their possession have been faithfully reproduced in the book." He rummages in his bag and says, "In fact, they emailed me a photo of Mr. Renard's portrait." He hands it to Rosen who compares it to the plate. It matches.

Mabry concludes: "The portraits were painted in the period from 1640-1680 and in fact, Ms. Renard's portrait is currently on view at the Met on loan from the British Library. I stopped by there before I came over."

Rosen covers his eyes and rubs his temples. He takes out the envelope with the photo of Charles. "Here's something else to ponder. This photo was taken by our photographer not quite a week ago."

Rosen places the photo beside the others. Mabry examines them closely.

"Oh my. They all match."

"I think you see my dilemma."

"I certainly do." Mabry rises and paces around the conference room then looks out into the squad room at a man and woman headed toward them. "And I also see them."

Rosen looks up to see Charles, accompanied by an attractive woman who resembles Carlotta, coming toward them. Charles knocks on the door and Rosen waves them in.

"Oh look, honey," Charles says. "They found some of our photos." Fox picks up the book with Carlton and Carlotta's picture then frowns and speaks in character. "Why did they use this one? We had much better pictures taken for this tour. Couldn't they have used the one where I was wearing my dark suit?"

"You looked positively smashing in that one, darling," Renee says in character.

Indicating Renee's photo, he says, "Of course, you look great in anything."

"Darling, you're making me blush."

"Okay we get it, you like each other," Rosen says. "You must be Renee."

"I am." Renee extends her hand.

"The guy staring in silent adoration is Dr. Mabry. He's a theater historian from Lincoln Center. He dug up all this material on you."

"Couldn't you have found better photos?" Fox asks indignantly, still in character.

Mabry nervously adjusts his glasses. "I only had a few days. I'm sure I could—"

"Charlie let it go." Renee takes the book from him. "Ignore him Dr. We know you didn't choose the photos for the book."

Rosen picks up the conference room phone and dials

the captain.

"Captain? Could you come to the conference room on one? There's something you need to see." He dials another number. "Joey? You got the Openshaw info? How about the fingerprint results? Great, bring them up."

While waiting, Dr. Mabry says, "Mr. Fox, if I may ask, the scar above your right eye, where did you get that?"

"I was appearing in a performance at the Globe. I was Laertes to Burbage's Hamlet."

"Richard Burbage?"

"The one and only. We'd occasionally switch back and forth in the roles, but he originated the lead. I got this during the fight scene at the end of one of the performances."

"He nicked you with his sword?" Mabry says excitedly.

"No, this man in the audience didn't think we were fighting hard enough and threw a bottle onto the stage from the upper level. It hit a beam and broke and a piece of it hit me here. I'm lucky the fool didn't take out the eye. The cut actually healed quickly, but I had to wear a bandage around for several days for appearance's sake."

"So, you knew Shakespeare?" Mabry says.

"We did," Renee says, "Lovely lady."

Mabry is caught off guard. "Are you saying Shakespeare was a woman?"

Charles and Renee exchange a look, and he says, "You haven't figured that out? It's in the plays, somewhat, but definitely in the Sonnets."

"There's lots of speculation," Mabry says.

"We were in the same room many times," Renee says.

"It turns out I do know someone who knew you when you were in Vaudeville," Rosen says. "Dennis Wiley."

Charles tells Renee, "We knew him as Denny — sharp kid, always on his toes."

"Ah. Denny. Yes." Renee giggles' "I suspect he may have had a slight crush on me. He was always a little giddy when I was around."

"How do you know him, Detective?"

"He's my great-uncle," Rosen says.

"You don't say," Renee says. "Is he still around?"

"Alive and almost as energetic as he was back then."

"We'd love to see him," Renee says.

"Absolutely!" Charles agrees. Pointing at Rosen. "Say, does he still have the coin I gave him?"

"He does," Rosen says with an emphatic nod. "He showed it to me the other day." He throws up his hands. "This is crazy. Uncle Denny is eighty-nine years old, and he knew you as adults when he was a kid."

Charles shrugs. "I stopped thinking about it a long time ago and just roll with it."

The captain enters and groans when he sees Charles. "I see Methuselah's back."

"I'm offended," Charles says indignantly, in character as Carlton. "I have a good seven hundred years on him."

"Not to mention you're a better kisser, darling," Renee adds, as Carlotta.

The captain waves his hand toward her. "And he brought a friend. How old are you supposed to be?"

Renee gives him a disgusted pout and responds in character. "Captain! A lady never reveals her age." She pauses. "Unless of course she's pushing fifteen hundred and looks as good as I do."

"Not an easy feat I might point out," Charles says as Carlton. "In fact, I'd say it's well nigh impossible."

"Darling, you're too kind," Renee says as Carlotta, fanning herself.

"Enough!" Rosen says. "Captain, I never thought I'd hear myself say this, but I think they're telling the truth. Not only do we have photographic evidence, but I know someone who knew them in the thirties, and he's verified their story."

He introduces Dr. Mabry, and they review all the information and photos.

Another detective with thinning hair and wearing a rumpled gray suit enters carrying a storage box. "Someone call for evidence?"

"Caputo, what are you doing here?" the captain says.

"1933 equals cold case. Though this one's getting warmer."

"Come on in, Joey," Rosen says.

Caputo sets the box on the end of the table. He takes out a file folder and removes two transparencies. He turns on the overhead projector.

"Okay, here we have the right index fingerprint from a male subject identified as Charles Fox, taken April 13, 1933." He places the transparency on the overhead. Once everyone's had time to see it, he takes the second one and says, "Right index print taken from subject Charles Fox July 12, 2005."

He lays the second transparency over the first and aligns them. They match. The captain shakes his head.

"So, who was this Fox guy? It says in the file he was ruled out as a suspect."

"Joe Caputo," Rosen says, motioning to Charles who gives a finger fluttering wave. "Charles Fox."

"This is a joke, right?"

"No joke," Tom says. "I was standing right there while they printed him."

Joe responds with a shrug. "Whatever."

Charles leans forward and says, "Was there mention of someone named Melvin?"

"Melvin?" Joe says then skims the witness and suspects list. "They questioned a Melvin Duggan who claimed to be a friend of Openshaw's. In fact, he's the one who called in with new info. He's supposed to be in this afternoon to make a statement. But how'd you guess that?"

"Detective, I rented the front room in William Openshaw's house for a few weeks in 1933," Charles says. "That's why they needed my fingerprints."

Joe looks from the captain to Rosen and back. "And you guys are buying this?"

Rosen shrugs. "You should take a look at some of these." He waves his hand over the books.

"So Duggan identified himself as a friend," Charles says out loud but mostly to himself.

"That's what he said," Caputo answers.

"Let's talk about the current killings," the captain says. "Caputo, you're here, so have a seat."

Joe sits and starts looking over the books and photos.

Renee addresses the captain. "We saw a news report

about them the other day and they seem to bear the mark of someone we know. A man named Bergeron."

"Someone like you," Rosen says.

"If you mean age-wise then yes," Renee says. "Beyond that, we have very little in common."

"He's a stone-cold killer," Charles continues. "He kills without hesitation and without remorse. If he hasn't killed you yet, it's quite possibly because he hasn't met you."

"His favorite targets over the past few centuries have been women," Renee says. "But don't let that fool you. He doesn't discriminate and he doesn't need a reason to kill. He enjoys it and has spent hundreds of years perfecting his technique. I'm sure you've heard of Vlad the Impaler."

Everyone nods or says, "Yeah."

"Bergeron most likely taught him the finer points of torture," she says. "Or at least they compared notes."

"Which brings us to Whitechapel." Charles glances toward the door and motions to someone. Rosen looks to see a small, red-headed woman enter. "Bergeron was there, he was dealing with the incompetence of a Victorian police force and there was really nothing stopping him. It would have been the perfect opportunity to really work out. But he got sidetracked."

"By what," Rosen says.

The red-haired woman answers. "By me."

The captain stands. "Victoria Wells."

"Hello again, Mike. Hope you're volunteering for the fundraiser this year. You were a big help last time."

"I wouldn't miss it. But how do you factor into all of this."

She closes the door behind her.

"I was all set to become the next victim of the Ripper after Mary Jane Kelly. Only he wasn't counting on me being able to do this."

She unwraps her scarf and opens the collar of her shirt.

Rosen, Caputo, and the captain exchange disturbed looks while Professor Mabry says, "Oh my!"

"Then you are—," the captain begins.

"Yes," Victoria says. "One hundred and sixty-seven

years old."

"You look really good for your age," Caputo says dryly.

Rosen whacks him on the arm.

"Thanks," Victoria says, sarcastically.

They talk for nearly an hour as the Foxes and Victoria tell them what they know about Bergeron.

"If you knew he was killing people," Caputo says, "then why didn't you tell anyone or try to stop him?"

Renee says, "Knowing something and proving it are two different matters."

Victoria adds, "She's right. For the Ripper killings I was the only evidence tying Bergeron to them. Do you imagine the local authorities would buy that I'd been killed by him? Also, Bergeron is very good at covering his tracks. I lived in his house for fourteen years and never realized he had started killing again until it was too late."

She turns to Charles and Renee. "But guys, it can't be Bergeron this time."

"Why do you say that?" Charles says.

"He's in prison. I put him there."

"And you're sure he's still there?" Renee says.

"He was when I checked at the end of last year, but I can contact the warden to check on him when I get back to my office."

"Great," Charles says. "We'll go with you."

When the discussion wraps up, the captain thanks Charles, Renee, Victoria and Professor Mabry and lets them go.

As they're walking through the squad room, a very old man with thinning white hair and a bit of a shuffling gait, accompanied by a young woman, pins his eyes on Charles and approaches.

The young woman seems caught off guard as she follows him. "Granddad?"

"Sir, do I know you?" the man says to Charles.

"I don't think so," Charles says.

"But you look so familiar," the old man says. "Is your family from New York?"

"No, not at all," Charles says.

The old man nods with a bit of a smile.

"A mistake on my part. Good day."

The young woman catches up to him and takes his arm. "Now Granddad, you shouldn't get away from me like that."

"I thought I recognized that gentleman," the old man says.

"Let's go sit down," the woman says.

They start toward the chairs, but Detective Caputo approaches them. Charles hears him say, "Are you Mr. Duggan?"

"Yes," the old man answers.

Charles spins about and takes a long look at the man.

"What is it, Charlie?" Renee says.

Charles nods his head toward the man and says to her, "Melvin."

She looks back at the man with a smile. "I guess he knew you after all."

Elle Rigby finishes making notes on the chart of a young boy in the critical care unit of Brooklyn Medical Center and replaces the chart at the foot of the bed. The boy was hit by a garbage truck while riding his bike in front of his home on Flatbush Avenue nearly a week ago, and while his condition was touch and go for several days, he now seems well on the road to making a full recovery. Elle pats his arm. "Sleep well, Dominic."

She heads back to the nurses' station where she catches up on her charting until the phone rings.

"Nurse Rigby, there's a Doctor Tremaine on the line for you."

"Francis Tremaine?" Eleanor says with a note of surprise in her voice.

"I believe so. Should I put him through?"

"Yes, please."

The line connects. "Hello, Elle. It's been a while."

"I would have to say, you are the last person I expected to call me out of the blue like this, Francis."

"Nice to speak to you, too, Elle." His voice sounds strained. "I took a chance you were still working in Brooklyn and made some calls — although your name change made it a bit challenging. How long have you been Eleanor Rigby?"

"Since the song came out. I liked the sound of it, plus it seemed appropriate given my circumstances."

"I hope you've been doing better than that."

"I'm doing what I love doing, Francis, helping others. I take it you're still practicing medicine."

"Mainly research, though I still dabble a bit in hands-on care."

"Well, I can't imagine you've looked me up after all this time just to shoot the breeze. How's Beth by the way?"

"Unfortunately, she's why I'm calling. Beth was in a very serious accident and she's in bad shape."

"Details?"

"The short version is that she was in a head-on collision and almost didn't make it. She's in a lot of pain, having trouble communicating, and has no memory of me or her life before the accident."

"That's horrible. How can I help?"

"Bethany needs a full-time caregiver. Live in."

Elle falls silent and takes in a deep breath.

"That won't be awkward at all."

"Look, I know things didn't end well for us and I'm sorry for that. But as you were always so fond of pointing out, we're not the most compatible as a couple."

"An understatement if ever I heard one."

"I imagine it will be a little touchy, but you're my only hope. It's not like there are a lot of people who'll understand our special circumstances. Plus, I need someone who speaks Celtic. It's currently the only way Beth can communicate."

Eleanor considers it a moment.

"You know I'd do anything for Bethany. I will always be grateful that she never took sides, despite her relationship with you. You're a doctor, I'm a nurse. If we agree to keep everything on a purely professional level, things should be manageable. I'm off at nine a.m. Can you pick me up?"

"I can."

"See you when you get here."

When Francis arrives, they go to a nearby diner she recommends.

"I want a full rundown of what I'll be encountering with Beth. Don't omit a single detail."

"I only have sketchy details from Beth's father-in-law and the New Jersey state trooper on what happened but judging by the damage to her, I'd guess the front of the car was demolished."

"What sort of car?"

"Late model station wagon."

"Who else was in it?"

"Her husband and kids. He died at the scene. The daughter and son were in the very back. Minor injuries. Treated and released from what I was told."

"So, then, neither one takes after their mother."

"That's my assumption. In fact I think I recall Beth stating they both had the flu last season."

"Those poor kids. Who's looking after them?"

"They're with their grandfather. You don't need to worry about them."

"You know me, Francis. I worry."

"You'll have enough worries with Beth. Her memory is completely gone. She doesn't know her name, how old she is, or where she came from."

"That bad."

"As far as she's concerned, her life began when she woke up and asked me who and where she was."

"You said she can only speak Celtic."

"She can hardly speak at all. Halting, incomplete phrases. But what she manages is in Celtic. I never understood why you felt the need to learn it, but I'm glad you did."

"I learned it so you and Beth couldn't talk about me when I was in the room with you."

"We didn't— Never mind."

After breakfast, Francis drives Elle back to his townhouse. Upstairs, outside one of the rooms, they're greeted by a nurse.

"Nurse Fletcher, this is El— Nurse Rigby. She's going to be taking over fulltime care of Miss Stone."

"Of course, Doctor. You've got your work cut out for you."

The three enter the room. Bethany is lying in bed, hooked up to an IV. Her expression is a mixture of confusion and trepidation. Her hair has been cut short and there are numerous scars on her face and head. When she sees Francis, she starts to speak in short, clipped sentences in Celtic. Elle steps to the bed and replies in the same language.

"My name is Eleanor. I am here to take care of you. You have nothing to worry about."

Bethany stares at Elle a moment, then nods.

"Are you in pain?"

Bethany raises her hand slightly and gestures across her body. "All. Hurt. Body."

Elle turns to Nurse Fletcher. "When did you last give her pain meds?"

"Shortly before you got here, so it should be kicking in about now. I've been varying the dosage hoping to find the best level to keep her comfortable but not groggy, but it's been very hit or miss. I don't think I've ever seen anyone in this shape who's still breathing."

Elle nods. "Yes. I know. I definitely want to study your charts."

"Certainly. I'll walk you through treatment when we get a spare second."

"Very good. Thank you so much for your work here, Nurse Fletcher. I can see Ms. Stone has been in good hands."

"The language barrier has been tough. My Mom is Haitian, so I grew up speaking French and I learned Spanish in school, but I have no idea what language this is. It's good you can communicate directly with her."

Elle pats Nurse Fletcher on the arm. "Why don't you take a breather now that I'm here. I'm sure you've earned it. Afterward, we can go over your notes."

"Thank you, Nurse Rigby."

Once she's gone, Elle turns to Bethany. "I need to speak to your doctor a few moments, then I'll be back to look after you."

Bethany gives her a slight smile and nods.

Elle and Francis step into the hallway.

"Ground rules: I am Nurse Rigby; you are Dr. Tremaine. We treat this exactly as we would a hospital situation."

"Fair enough."

"Also, I want to know everything you know about Beth's family."

"To what purpose?"

"For my own peace of mind. How's that?"

"All right. But I don't want you rushing to their aid. Last I checked, they seemed to be in good hands with their grandfather. Also, I'm planning to send them some funds."

"Really?"

"Yes. I'm just trying to work out how best to get it to Mr. Morelli without arousing his suspicions too much."

"Good luck with that. Okay, then. If you're not just cutting them off, that makes me feel a little better about the situation."

"As of now, as far as the world is concerned, Bethany Morelli is dead, so I'm going to start calling her by a new name. Her father-in-law and children don't need to know what actually happened. The person they know is pretty much gone, so it's best they be allowed to move on with their lives."

"Under the circumstances, I find it very difficult to argue with that approach."

"It's good that you're here, Elle — that is, Nurse Rigby. I suspect we'll have to play most of this by ear anyway."

"I agree, Dr. Tremaine. Now, if you'll excuse me, I have a patient to attend to. Please let Nurse Fletcher know I'll be down shortly once Beth drops off to sleep."

Elle steps back into the room and takes a seat beside the bed. Bethany appears a bit more relaxed.

"Nurse Fletcher says she gave you something for the pain. How are you feeling?"

Bethany considers it. "Hurt. Not. Bad."

"Good. I'm here and I'm not going anywhere, so let me know if there's anything you need."

Dennis Wiley is reading the paper in the activity room of his senior living community. He hears his name and looks to see his grandnephew Tom entering.

"Tommy! Twice in one week? You're making me feel special."

"You are special Uncle Denny."

"To what do I owe the pleasure?"

"I brought a couple of folks with me who wanted to say hello. Come on in you two."

Charles and Renee step into the door then Charles takes Renee's hand and twirls her, and they do a tango toward Dennis then strike a pose, side by side with their arms extended, knees bent slightly. Dennis stares at them a moment then removes his glasses and cleans them and puts them back on.

"Renee? Charlie?"

"How you doing, Denny?" Charles walks over and pats him on his shoulder. Renee bends down and gives him a hug.

"Man, I thought I looked good for my age. You two take the cake."

"Rosen says you still have that coin I gave you," Charles says. "Glad to hear you never hit a rough patch."

"Times would have to be awfully tough for me to part with that, but what's up with you two? You haven't changed a bit since I saw you, what, sixty-five or seventy years ago?"

"We're just luckier than most," Renee says.

Dennis nods then leans forward with his eyes narrowed and points a finger. "How can I be sure you're not two look-a-likes just pulling a fast one on me. Tommy here could have filled you in on my history."

Suddenly dropping into character as Carlotta, Renee looks at Charles with a wide-eyed smile. "Darling, we have a skeptic in the audience!"

Charles crosses his arms and leans toward her then responds as Carlton. "Well, Dear, we'll just have to erase all doubts."

Recognizing the characters, Dennis sits back with a wide grin on his face. Rosen sits beside him. Some of the residents start to assemble around where they're gathered.

"Do that routine you used to do to open the shows," Dennis says.

They confer in whispers, then start with a soft-shoe routine, dancing side by side in unison. They twirl then slide past one another and resume dancing in unison. A small crowd starts to gather. As they warm up, Charles says, "What was the song we used, Silvery moon?"

Renee shakes her head and shrugs.

"I remember!" Dennis says. He sings a few bars moving his hand in time with the music. "Picture you upon my knee—"

"Ah yes!" Renee says. "With tea for two and two for tea." They start singing as they dance, and the small crowd of residents grows a bit larger. When they get to the line "a boy for you and a girl for me," Charles and Renee point to one another on "boy" and to themselves on "girl" then exchange confused looks which elicits a few laughs. They conclude by dropping to one knee with both arms extended. First Charles' left arm is in front of Renee's right arm, but she moves her arm in front of his and he does the same and they continue this for a few moments, glaring at one another as the crowd snickers then finally they look back to the crowd with overly earnest smiles. The crowd claps.

Dennis sits back, wagging his finger at Renee and Charles. "Now that you can't fake. Renee I'd love to hear you sing something."

"I'd love for you to hear me sing. But who could I get to accompany me on the piano?"

Someone in the audience says, "Mrs. Miller plays."

A small Black woman comes out of the crowd and goes to the piano with Renee. "Do you know 'All of Me'?"

"I certainly do." Mrs. Miller plays a few bars.

"That's the one."

Mrs. Miller plays the introduction and Renee comes in. Listening, Dennis leans over to Rosen. "What did I tell you — the voice of an angel."

Renee finishes and the crowd claps. Charles whispers

something to Mrs. Miller and she nods then he steps over to a man seated nearby with a cane and wearying a homburg.

"Sir, could I borrow your hat and cane a moment? I swear I'll bring them back in the same condition."

The man hands Charles the requested items and he puts the hat on, straightens the collar of his coat, and strikes a pose, holding the cane against his chest, and tipping the hat.

"Ready when you are Mrs. Miller."

She begins playing Puttin' on the Ritz and Charles sings and does a dance routine, using the cane to tap the floor or twirl. As he finishes, he spins around to the man who loaned him the props and hands over the cane placing the hat back on the man's head.

They remain at the center for nearly two hours entertaining the residents. At the end, the director, who came in about halfway through the performance suggests they come back again, to which Renee and Charles enthusiastically agree.

Theresa Morelli taps on the door of the nurse's office on the first floor of her high school near her home room. She hears an unfamiliar voice saying, "Come in," enters, but pauses when she sees it's not the regular nurse she visits.

"Oh. You're not Patty."

The brown-haired woman tilts her head with a bit of a grin. "Right. I'm Nurse Goolsby. Patty isn't feeling well today and I was on-call."

"Hi. I'm Theresa. Me and Patty usually have a monthly get together. You know, around that time of the month."

"Yes. I did see a note stating that you might stop in."

Theresa has the odd feeling she's met Nurse Goolsby before. She examines her closely.

"Is everything all right?"

"Do you go by another name? I mean, is this, like, your married name?"

"This is the name I was born with."

Theresa chuckles and takes a seat in front of the desk.

"I'm sorry. It's just that for a minute, I was sure I've met you before, but I can't remember where that might have been. I thought if I knew you by another name, that might remind me."

"Ah. Yes. I have one of those faces. Someone mistook me for Stephanie Zimbalist once, but I'm not sure who that is."

"I think she's on television. Remington Steele maybe. I don't watch the show."

"I don't watch television, so guess that explains that. Anyway, I did look over your file and I'll have to remember to thank Patty for taking such great notes. I feel like we are well acquainted now — at least from my perspective. You're a senior, correct?"

"I am."

"I'll bet you're looking forward to graduating."

"Definitely."

Nurse Goolsby retrieves a file from a stack on the desk and opens it.

"I just need to confirm a few facts then I can get your supplies and let you be on your way." She reads over the information. "I understand you're living with your grandfather and that both your parents are deceased."

"That's right. It's sort of why I've been coming to see Patty. I think my grandpa is a bit uncomfortable dealing with these types of women's concerns."

"Totally understandable. I lost most of my family at a relatively young age as well, so I can sympathize."

"That's terrible. How did you deal with it?"

"In some ways, I'm still dealing with it, but the best advice is day by day."

"Yeah. I'm certainly doing that."

"Good to hear. How old were you when you lost them? If you don't mind my asking."

"No. That's okay. Early teens. Just a few years ago in fact. What about you?"

"I was maybe a little younger than you were, actually. Although I never really knew my father."

"Well, I did. I miss them both, but especially my Mom."

"You were close?"

Theresa nods. "She was my best friend."

"That's good to hear. I wasn't always so close with mine."

She looks over the file. "I'm going to go out on a limb and say you're not married and have no kids."

Theresa hesitates. "No. I'm not married."

Nurse Goolsby looks up. "I'm sensing there's a 'but' coming."

Theresa considers it a long moment. "Anything I tell you is a secret, right?"

"Of course."

"Because nobody knows this. Not even Patty."

"Knows what?"

"A few years ago, I had a kid. A girl."

"Really. How old were you?"

"It was when I was a sophomore. I wasn't in school at the time. It was over the summer."

"I see. You don't really need to tell me about it. This is all just routine."

"I know. But I've wanted to tell somebody. Well, somebody outside my family. I can't talk to any of my friends about it, or my teachers or coaches. And you're just here for a day or so and I'll probably never see you again."

"Never say never, but I think I understand. And I'm a good listener."

"I just wonder if I did the right thing. I mean, I was pretty sure I couldn't take care of her. And the family who adopted her was really nice. I could tell they loved her, and they'd do right by her. I guess what I really regret is that I didn't have Mom around to talk to about it. I know she would have given me the best advice. I tried to do what I think she'd have wanted me to do."

Nurse Goolsby takes it all in, then grasps Theresa's hand.

"I think, if your mother was here, she'd be proud of the way you've handled the situation. Once you knew you couldn't care for the child, you made sure she was placed with a loving family who would give her a wonderful life. The fact that you still think about her is ample evidence of your concern for her."

"I think, on some level, I know that. But I'll never stop thinking about her. Hoping that someday, I'll get to see how she turned out."

"It's always a possibility. But if not, you should trust that you did the best you could under difficult circumstances. That's all anyone can expect."

Theresa considers this. "Yeah. You're probably right. I'm kind of glad Patty wasn't here today." She laughs. "Don't tell her I said that."

"Your secrets are safe with me. All of them."

Douglas Mabry is in his office at Lincoln Center, when someone taps on his door.

"Come in."

He's surprised that it's Renee Fox and she has a package with her.

"Ms. Fox. This is a surprise."

"Now, professor, what did I tell you last time we talked?" She gives him a quick hug.

"Sorry, Renee. What brings you here?" He motions to a chair next to his desk where she sits.

"I've brought you a gift." She sets the package on his desk. "Charlie and I have been doing some spring cleaning and we keep running across all these items we didn't know we had or that we have more than we need, or just plain don't need anymore."

"I suspect you'd rival Oxford University for the number of things stored in your attic."

"That's an understatement, professor. Anyway, while we were going through things from the Elizabethan period, we found an old trunk and it was filled with some of our items from around that time and this was one of them."

She opens the package and carefully removes a very old manuscript with a leather cover, held together by leather straps at several places along the spine. Mabry puts on a pair of gloves and opens it. The pages are yellow but in relatively good shape. The typeset is like an Elizabethan era printing press, but there are handwritten notations throughout. The title page reads: The Most Excellent and Lamentable Tragedy of Romeo and Juliet.

Mabry examines it with fascination. "Is this a script?"

"It's a prompt book."

"A prompt book?" Mabry's excitement rises.

"Yes. As you can see this one's for Romeo and Juliet. Someone in the company would have had it in the box at the foot of the stage and whenever an actor got off track, the person in the box could prompt him with the next line. Since women weren't allowed on the stage during Elizabeth's time, I ended up doing this a lot, which is probably how I ended up with this one. I did sneak on-stage a few times when no one was paying attention."

Mabry examines the pages. "I don't think I've ever seen one this complete from that era. We assumed they'd all been destroyed or lost."

"Most have been, but Charlie and I tend to be pack-rats when it comes to certain items."

Mabry has a thought. "Whose handwriting is this?"

Renee looks over the pages. She points to a quickly scribbled notation in the text. "The shorthand is mine. Sometimes when the play was new, the actors would toss in a line or two or say a line differently than was written and if it worked better, that would stay in." She points to the neater notations. "These are from the playwright who'd make last minute changes as she saw how each line or direction played out."

"Shakespeare? This is a prompt-book that has Shakespeare's own notations in it?"

"Yes it is." She looks over the manuscript. "These are Emmie's notations."

"I'm still trying to wrap my head around the authorship news you gave me at our last encounter." Mabry sits back in his chair. "I've reread the Sonnets and many of the plays, and I'm finding it hard to dispute what you told me. You understand, Renee, I'll have to get this authenticated."

"I'd expect you to. In fact, I suggest you get second and third opinions."

"We'll do just that. But surely you're not just giving this to us."

"Why not? We have plenty of them."

"You do? How many?"

Renee considers this. "Well, I know we have Hamlet and Othello — those are two of Charlie's favorites. In fact, we have three different versions of Hamlet and several of the comedies. At least one of the history plays." She shrugs. "I'd have to go through the trunk."

"I assume you know how valuable those must be."

"Professor Mabry. At the dawn of the twentieth century Charles and I owned several thousand acres of land in and around London, Middlesex, and Kent. We sold all but a few parcels over the course of the century — whenever the market was right. It's the same with Paris. Not only that, but we've been collecting artwork over the course of a thousand years and selling it whenever we either got tired of it or wanted to pare down the collection. That's not to mention salaries we've made as actors, educators or whatever else we did for a living as well as investments, some of which have been earning interest for as long as there have been banks to pay it. I assure you we don't need the money."

"No, I imagine not." He picks up his phone. "Gloria? Would you ask the director to come down here, please? He is? Well, interrupt them. Yes, I'll take full responsibility."

A short while later, the director of Mabry's section comes in looking angry.

"Mabry, I hope this is important."

"This is Renee Fox. She's making a donation to the center."

"What sort of donation?"

Mabry sweeps his hand over the prompt book. "Take a look."

The director puts on a pair of white gloves and looks through the manuscript.

"Is this what I think it is?"

"If you think it's a prompt book from the Globe Theater with Shakespeare's own notations in it then yes, it is," Renee says.

He closes it and gives Renee and Mabry a skeptical look.

"How do we know this is real?"

"You tell me," Renee says. "I'll leave the authentication up to you. Use whoever you want."

The director is suddenly seized with a fit of laughter. "If this is genuine, it's one of a kind. I doubt the Folger Library has one of these. I don't even think you can put a value on it."

He removes his gloves and drops them on the desk.

"Mabry, this is just the sort of thing I like being interrupted to see."

"I thought you wouldn't mind."

As much as he hates saying goodbye, Roland knows the time has come. He's spent more than a century in his adopted homeland of Australia, but now he's decided to take a friend up on an offer which he knows he shouldn't refuse. As it is, he's several years late, though this particular friend won't mind the extra time. Hearing the blast of a horn, he looks to see his cohort Trevor pulling up in Roland's cab.

"How's she suit you?"

Trevor gives him two thumbs up. "She's a beaut. Are you sure you want to get rid of her? This one's still got a lot of miles left in her."

"I'm sure, Trev. Too much hassle to take with, plus I know you'll take as good a care of her as I would."

"You can bet on that, my friend." They shake hands.

"Now how about collecting your first fare, eh?" Roland lifts his suitcase.

"Sure thing, sir." Trevor speaks in a mock-deferential tone. "Where you headed?"

"Airport."

"No worries. We'll have you there straight away."

Trevor drops Roland at the terminal at Sydney International Airport and gives him a hug.

"Guess you're really going through with it after all."

"I am. But no worries, Trev, I'll check in once in a while."

"You better." Trevor pats his shoulder.

Roland heads inside to the ticket counter.

"Yes sir?" the ticket agent says.

"Roland Fox, checking in."

The attendant types. "One way to New York City."

"That's the one."

She prints his ticket. "Have a nice trip, sir."

"Indeed I will."

Proof Positive

www.ingramcontent.com/pod-product-compliance
Lightning Source LLC
Chambersburg PA
CBHW031420250626
47155CB00004B/1560

* 9 7 8 0 9 9 8 1 5 9 5 9 1 *

Bishopsgate, London, Christmas Eve, 2005: Daniel Seely sits at the kitchen table reading The London Times. He looks across at his wife Martha, who's smearing strawberry jam onto some toast.

"What time are Donald and Harriett arriving?"

"Around noon." She takes a bite.

"It'll be good to see the little ones again." He glances over the lead story. "Too bad Billy can't make it."

"Speaking of which, has the postman been here? I'm expecting a card from Billy."

Daniel looks up from his paper. "I believe I did hear him."

He goes out to the box. Inside is an envelope with no return address and the words, "Do not bend!" on the outside. The postmark is from New York. He takes the envelope back to the dining room.

"Just the one letter, dear. Not from our son."

"Who's it from?"

"Doesn't say. It's from America, though."

"Who do we know in America?"

"Let's find out."

He opens the envelope and removes a Christmas card. Inside is a check for £10,000 made out to the Seely Family Association and a photo of two women with light red hair, one taller than the other, who appear to be related. Martha stares at the check then looks back to the photo.

"Do you know these women?"

He points to the taller one. "I recognize this one. I believe that's Allison Stepney."

"The clothing designer?"

"Yes, I told you I met her once some years ago. She was inquiring about the family. She doesn't appear to have changed much since then. I don't know who this other one is, though they look like sisters."

"Is anything written on back?"

He flips the photo over and reads: "Dear Daniel, All the evidence you need, from your great-great-grandaunts, Victoria and Sarah." He puzzles over this. "What the devil does that mean?"